Diondray's Discovery

(Diondray's Chronicles Book 1)

Marion Hill

Chapter 1

I drove on Ama's Way, headed to my family's home. It had been three years since I'd been on this road and this side of Charlesville. I opened the windows of my automobile and let the breeze from the Bay of Charlesville refresh me.

I looked out at the sea and realized how much it reminded me of those days from my childhood when I would spend hours throwing small rocks into the water and playing along the beach with my friends. The Bay of Charlesville had become my companion during family arguments and issues.

Since it was day four in the month of Beru, the second month of the year, I felt the breeze from the bay. This was the coldest area of the city. Charlesville was hot and muggy most of the time, and many people valued living on the east side in order to get that breeze.

I arrived at my family's home. I was pleased that the main gate still opened for me automatically. I had thought my rebellious action would cause me to be treated like a guest upon my arrival instead of as an Azur.

I didn't want to return here. My mother had pleaded with me for several months to come. She'd promised to keep everyone in line and to do everything in her power to have a nice evening with her only child. I had agreed to come, but I sensed that all the issues that caused me to leave would rear their ugly heads again.

I took a couple of deep breaths after I parked. I hoped I would have a nice birthday dinner with my family and leave as soon as possible.

"The wayward son has returned home," Uncle Xavier said as I sat down at the dining table.

I saw the look of satisfaction his face. I'd known that look since childhood. It said, *I'm the ruler of Charlesville, and don't you forget your place.* His blow-out hairstyle looked like a perfectly cut treetop and accentuated his night-colored skin. Uncle Xavier's long, thin fingers, covered with gold rings on each hand, hit the table after his comment. He did that at every family dinner.

"So how do you like living amongst the ants?" he asked.

"They are not ants, Uncle Xavier," I replied. "Don't forget you represent all the citizens of Charlesville, not just those who live next to the sea."

"Diondray! Don't speak to your Uncle Xavier like that. He is the ruler of our city and should be shown a little more respect," my mother interjected.

I faced my mother, already feeling the anger I had dreaded in coming back home. Olivia Azur was my uncle's biggest defender and supporter. I supposed being his older sister, she always believed her role was to protect her little brother.

Even though my mother could never be ruler, she was the one who kept everything concerning the city together. Her sharp mind and steadiness also kept Uncle Xavier in line. He knew he could not continue his rule without my mother at his side and accepted her role as his protector.

"Why doesn't he respect those people who live on the west side like he does the people who live out here? Aren't they citizens too?"

"My son, Xavier was just having a little small talk with you.

Remember, it's your birthday. Let's enjoy the evening."

I had to calm down. If I didn't, I would end up walking away from the dinner table. I had dreaded being here, and I realized our family dinners had not changed since I left home three years ago.

"Watch your tongue!" Uncle Xavier said in a condescending tone.

Aunt Maxina cut in. "Xavier and Olivia, you two can't help yourselves, can you? You invited my nephew back here to celebrate his birthday, and now both of you are chastising him about living on the west side. Shameful."

Aunt Maxina's comments surprised me. She was usually the quiet one and let my mother and Uncle Xavier dominate the discussion. I'd always thought she zoned us out and entered into her own little world. She always had a look of peacefulness on her face. Her big brown eyes, which covered most of her face, would fixate on either my mother or Uncle Xavier like she wanted to hypnotize them. Aunt Maxina would let them talk, and every time I looked at her, I felt she had not heard a word they had said.

Until now.

"Thanks, Aunt Maxina," I replied and smiled at her.

She smiled in return, and I felt comforted. Even though she had always seemed distant, I believed that she'd never had a problem with me leaving home.

"Yes, sister, you are right. Xavier and I should have not created any tension with Diondray. He is still an Azur even if we don't agree with how he has decided to live his life."

"Willar, please bring our dinner," Uncle Xavier commanded and glared at me.

Willar, the family servant, brought dinner to the table. He looked the same as when I left. About an inch or so taller than me, skinny as a pencil, with a similar complexion to myself. People here on the east side sometimes suggested he was my dad. Mother scoffed at that perception. She would never stoop so low as to be romantically involved with the help.

Willar was dressed like we had an official city function. A sun-yellow shirt with pressed black pants and a thick yellow stripe on the outside of each pant leg made him resemble one of the CRG guards.

"Welcome back, Diondray," he said in his baritone voice while setting the plates at the table. "I made your favorite dinner."

"Thanks, Willar."

He pulled the cover off my plate, and I caught the irresistible smell of bluefish. The bluefish took up most of the plate, but Willar had placed cut slices of mango bread around it in a circle.

"How is life on the west side?" he asked while pulling covers off the rest of the family plates.

"Very well, Willar. They care about their neighborhoods and welcomed me as one of their own."

"Really? I guess ants do stick together."

I shot a look at my uncle as he and my mother laughed.

"Well, I'm glad you enjoy living there. I will return shortly with dessert," Willar said and left.

"Xavier, will you stop!" Aunt Maxina said.

"Stop what, my sister? I'm the ruler of Charlesville and have the right to speak my mind. My nephew thinks he is noble, living amongst the ants and trying to act like he is one of the common folk. Why doesn't he tell them the reason he can live there without having to work is because of the family he belongs to?"

"Xavier, please!" my mother pleaded.

"No, sister! This boy needs to learn whom he belongs to and start appreciating his position in life. And reading some fancy words to those ants doesn't make him a more caring person."

"I knew this was a bad idea. I didn't come here to get lectured by him." I rose from the table.

"Sit down, boy. You are still an Azur."

"Uncle Xavier, I'm not a boy. Do you forget I'm twenty-three years old and a man who can make his own decisions?"

"You're twenty-three, really! You need to grow up before I can call you a man."

"I don't live here and never will while you are the ruler of this city," I said and began walking away from the dinner table.

"Diondray, I'm sorry," Aunt Maxina called after me.

"Don't leave, my son."

"Good-bye, family," I said and left.

Chapter 2

I thought about my uncle's comments from last night. It still bothered me that he called the people who live on this side of the city *ants.* It also bothered me that he thought I didn't appreciate my position as a member of the Azur family.

I'd always been aware of my status and never wanted to dismiss that or hide it. I was happy to represent myself as an Azur. But I would not do it by living in my family home and refusing to interact with all of the city's citizens.

I should have declined my mother's invitation and stayed away from that place. I did spend some time next to the sea after I left the house. It was calming to see the tide crashing against the beach, and the gurgling sound of the waves got my mind away from dinner.

I pulled back the fabric that covered the windows of my rented flat. I saw children playing stickball in the street and families walking by on the sidewalk and wondered why Uncle Xavier spoke with such contempt toward these people. These were good-hearted, hardworking people who loved this city and wanted to be treated fairly as citizens.

Did Uncle Xavier have a problem with the influx of people who had come from Terrance since the Year 175 A.O.A.? It had been thirty years of immigration, and their influence on the west side was quite evident. I'd noticed the difference even since I've lived here for the past three years.

The immigrants had brought their sense of style to our city, wearing plaid shirts with thick collars and *shorts.*. The men had their hair cut low to the scalp and were even bald much of the time, and the women wore their hair thinner and wilder than the natives of Charlesville did. It reminded me of the string pasta I used to eat growing up.

More radically, they didn't believe in the life charts the native-born citizens of Charlesville used. At first, that created conflict between the two groups. But time had healed that divide, and over the last thirty years both groups had mixed their beliefs to create a new kind of spiritual system. Many east siders, including my mother and uncle, believed the people of the west side were desecrating the life charts and Ama with this mixing of spiritual systems.

Uncle Xavier thought he didn't have anything in common with the immigrants, and he wanted to stop the policy Great-Uncle Myro had put in place back in the Year 175 A.O.A. Great-Uncle Myro wanted to increase the labor pool and grow the city at the same time. He knew the population of Charlesville had to grow in order for it to become a vital city in the future. He wanted immigrants from Terrance to work in Charlesville Bay as fishermen and take other jobs associated with the sea trade. He worked with Syonne, governor of Terrance at that time, and both men thought it would be a win-win proposition for both cities. They signed an initial twenty-year agreement for the immigration, and a relationship was born between the two cities. Well, Syonne didn't let his best citizens migrate to Charlesville. He allowed the pariahs and outcasts to come here. Tension grew between the rulers. But Syonne told Great-Uncle Myro that he would send better citizens if they renewed the agreement.

Great-Uncle Myro honored the agreement for the full period and was willing to sign a renewal because of the success the initial immigrants brought to the sea trade, even if they weren't the kind of people he'd wanted at first. Uncle Xavier pleaded with Great-Uncle Myro not to renew the agreement since he was next in line to be the ruler of the city and was afraid the immigrants would overpopulate Charlesville.

Great-Uncle Myro appeased his son publicly, but privately he continued the agreement for another ten years. As a result, Charlesville's sea trade became the best in all the region south of the Great Forest. Uncle Xavier was incensed when he found out about the secret renewal agreement after Great-Uncle Myro died. Mother told me that from that moment, he despised immigrants who lived on the west side.

*　*　*

I arrived at Aliki Park later that morning. I'd had a restless night of sleep. Aliki Park was the city's largest park and one of the few places in Charlesville where residents from both sides of the city came together and could enjoy each other's company.

I would come here every chance I got when I lived back at the family home. There was always something going on, from dances to playing stickball to cook-offs. And the fact that both west siders and east siders put down their differences made it worth the opposition I endured from Mother to come to the park.

The sun had risen, and it was already hot. I felt the sweat trickling down my back, and my throat was getting parched. Nine o'clock in the morning didn't spare us from the Charlesville heat.

I prepared myself to deliver today's themily. A *themily* was a collection of thoughts written on a single sheet of paper that were meant to inspire, encourage, or admonish the audience. Themily readings were one of the most popular events at the park, and some of the best readers had become well-known throughout the west side.

Themily readings were started by the immigrants when they came to the city. The readings kept them connected to their former home, and some of the early immigrants became so successful through their readings that they were able to return to Terrance.

Mother thought writing words on a piece of paper and reading them to people was a waste of my talent—and not only that, but it didn't honor the teachings of my life chart. When she found out I was doing themily readings, she forbade me to come to Aliki Park.

I explained to her how themily readings inspired people. I told her how the looks on the faces of the audience made me feel alive and recognized for the first time in my life. It didn't matter to Mother. My life chart said I was to be a ruler, next in line after Uncle Xavier, and rulers didn't read words at a park to common folk. Well, I kept coming to the park, defying her order. That decision led me on the path of leaving the family home. As I stood in the park feeling the heat and preparing to read, I thought again that it had been one of the best decisions I'd made in my life.

* * *

"Life is like a tropical storm coming each year. You don't know when exactly it's coming. But you have a sense it will come. And you have to be prepared in order to survive it," I announced to my audience at the park.

"That's weak, Mr. Azur," shouted a man from the audience. He wore a brown shirt with the thickest plaid stripes I had ever seen. "We have a tropical storm every year in the months of Une and Berm."

The audience roared in laughter. He was right. Our tropical storm season began in the month of Une, the sixth month, and continued until Berm, the ninth month. As Charlesville citizens, we expected at least one tropical storm a year.

"What else do you have, Mr. Azur?" the same man asked.

I chuckled at his remark. Everyone knew when the tropical storm season came, I guessed they wanted a little more from my themily. "Patience is not only a virtue. But a gift to those who've learned how to master it."

"Weak again," my critic replied. "You don't master patience, Mr. Azur. Either you are born with it or you are not."

The audience roared again. They liked the fact that my critic was getting the best of me. I had spent fourteen days on this themily, and it was shot down in matter of minutes. The audience at the park could be harsh if a themily reading didn't go well.

"What's wrong, Mr. Azur?" a woman asked. She wore a sky-blue, one-piece outfit and stood in the closest row to the podium. "You are usually pretty good at these readings for an east sider—especially one who belongs to the city's main family. Do you have something else on your mind?"

"Patience only works if you are wealthy," another person blurted.

"Ask Xavier if he can teach all of his citizens how to be patient," another person commented.

The audience continued with their comments on how bad my themily was, and I wanted to shrink from that podium and just go home.

"All right, everybody, that's enough. Brother Diondray doesn't deserve that kind of treatment. He has given excellent themily readings over time, and what he just read has some merit," Trayvonne announced as he joined me at the podium.

The audience calmed down and began leaving the podium. It was amazing to see how Trayvonne Filleu could handle a crowd. It seemed like he could get people in a trance and make them do whatever he said.

"C'mon, bro," he said to me.

I followed him off the podium and began to feel somewhat better.

"What happened?" I said as we both walked through the park. Why had the reading been such a disaster?

"It happens to all of us, bro. Sometimes the audience will reject your themily even if you have read good ones in the past," he replied as we reached a bench.

"It felt different, Trayvonne. Like I didn't belong in front of them."

Trayvonne flashed his wide, reassuring smile at me and sat down on the bench. "Bro, don't forget what family you belong to. There will always be distance between the common folk and yourself."

I felt anger rise in me. "So I'm the novelty act for this audience?"

He laughed as he placed a hand on my shoulder. "At first, yes, you were. But you have proven yourself to the west siders. We know you are not hanging around and living amongst us just to make yourself feel noble. We know you don't view us as ants. The people are just being difficult today for the fun of it."

I appreciated his honesty as he laughed. He knew how much I hated the term *ants*. People should never be compared to insects, and if Uncle Xavier ever came around here to see these folks, he would never see them in such a derogatory manner.

Trayvonne patted down his blow-out hairstyle. It was the largest I'd ever seen, big even for the west side. It was large enough that birds could nest in there. I wished I could grow mine as large as his.

"You will have another shot tomorrow, bro. I promise that the audience will be different."

"Sure about that?" I said as a woman arrived at the bench.

"Trust me," he replied as he got up from the bench to embrace the woman. "Portia, say hello to my bro, Diondray Azur."

"Hello," she said and smiled at me.

I recognized Portia from the reading. She was the woman in the sky-blue outfit. I should have known she was associated with Trayvonne. He never lacked for female company and always got the best of what the west side had to offer.

I waved back as they turned to walk away. Trayvonne patted her voluptuous behind, and she giggled. I just shook my head and hoped tomorrow's reading would be better.

* * *

"What's in the dark will always come to the light. Things can only stay in the dark for so long. Eventually the light will find its way through," I said from the podium.

I noticed the head nodding and smiles of agreement on the faces in the audience. I took that as a positive sign after yesterday.

"That's right, Mr. Azur."

I searched the audience for that voice and saw my critic from yesterday smiling at me in agreement. I didn't think I was going to win him over so quickly.

"That's why it's important to stick with the truth," I continued. "The truth can reveal. The truth can expose. The truth can hurt. And the truth can lead to freedom."

"Right on, Mr. Azur. Truth is freedom."

The audience clapped, to my surprise. I didn't know I had won them over so quickly. I'd thought they were going to mark me as a bad themily reader and it would take several readings to get their approval back.

I glanced to the right of the podium, where Trayvonne and Portia were smiling at me. He was right again. I should have known by now to trust him. He had a connection to these people unlike anything I had ever witnessed before. I wished our family could connect to these people like that.

I had more to read, but the audience had already begun leaving.

I'd recovered from yesterday's reading, and they'd only needed those few words at the beginning in order to give their approval. I was not marked. A relief.

I stepped off the podium and was greeted by Trayvonne and Portia.

"Trust me, bro," Trayvonne said with a wink. He was holding Portia, who was wearing a solid pink outfit. I nodded. "Of course, you were right."

"That was really good, Diondray," Portia remarked.

"Thank you."

"That was good, my nephew."

I looked over to the left of Portia to see where that comment came from. "Aunt Maxina, what are you doing here?"

"I had to see for myself. I hated the way Xavier and Olivia treated you at your birthday dinner. I wanted to see you in your element."

She had a look of affirmation on her face. No one from my family had ever come see me do a themily reading. And for Aunt Maxina to show up was especially surprising.

Trayvonne patted my shoulder as he and Portia left, arm in arm. Aunt Maxina and I stood there and watched them walk away.

"Your message about the truth touched me," she said. "I have to show you something about our family that you need to know."

Chapter 3

I didn't hear from Aunt Maxina for ten days after the surprise visit to Aliki Park. Then she called one night to say what time we would meet in the morning. She mentioned again how those words from the themily reading had touched her.

I arrived at Ama's Faddar just after the sun rose. Aunt Maxina had said on the phone that morning would be the best time to have full access to the building.

Ama's Faddar was the spiritual home of the city and the tallest building in Charlesville. It towered over all the other buildings, and its position on Ama's Way, next to the Bay of Charlesville, made it feel remote and impenetrable.

A cylindrical building, Ama's Faddar had an opening on the top floor, called Ama's Lookout. That was where the *oraki*, the city's spiritual leader, went to pray to Ama, the God of the Sky and Stars.

The oraki had a direct connection to Ama and communicated his instructions and teachings to the people of the city. He had the responsibility four times a year of taking the life charts from every newborn in the city and praying to Ama for his blessing and their fulfillment.

The oraki held up those life charts through the opening at the top of the tower and remained until Ama brought his essence down from the sky to bless it. He could remain for days or even months, waiting on Ama.

I arrived at the main entrance at the bottom of the building where Aunt Maxina was waiting for me. She was dressed in a black shawl with gold trimming. Aunt Maxina smiled as she handed me a shawl.

I pulled the shawl over my clothes. It was a sign of respect for Ama. Nobody entered Ama's Faddar without a shawl. It could have brought misfortune to that person and their family for such a disrespectful act.

"How did you get full access to Ama's Faddar?" I asked as we entered.

She shot me an incredulous look. "Aren't we the Azur family?

"Yes."

"There is nothing in this city off-limits to us," she replied.

"I thought only the oraki had access in here," I said as looked around on the ground floor.

I had never been inside of Ama's Faddar, and the curiosity I felt about this place only grew as I took in the reality around me. The walls were black from floor to ceiling, and tiny yellow lights like stars covered the entire area. I felt like I had entered into space.

"I have thought about your reading since we last met. I didn't know you could speak so eloquently, purposefully, and passionately."

"Thanks."

"Those people were captivated by your words," she continued as we reached an elevator. "The truth does bring freedom, my nephew."

I nodded as we entered the elevator. "Are we going to Ama's Lookout?" I asked.

"No, my nephew," she answered sharply. "That's the only place in the city we don't have access to. We are going to another room. There is something you must see."

We exited the elevator and walked a short distance to the end of the hallway. She rubbed gingerly on the door, and it opened.

The room looked similar to the main room downstairs. However, there was a podium in the center of the room that had glass encircling it.

"What is that?"

"The truth, my nephew," she said and pulled open the glass. "This is the Book of Kammbi."

The words meant nothing to me. "The Book of Kammbi?"

"This book reveals a part of our history that has never been talked about before. And as you said so eloquently, the truth is freedom."

She handed me the Book of Kammbi. It looked old and worn. The cover was the same color as the walls, and the book felt like it could rip apart at any moment.

"I believe that book will change our city's destiny, and you will be responsible for that change," she said. "Our history as a family has not been told completely."

"What do you mean?" I asked as I returned the book to her.

I stared at Aunt Maxina and tried to read her face. Did she understand the implications of what she had just said? I knew our history. Charles Azur and Mother Adrianna, were the ancestors who founded our city and began our family's rule. The city was named after Charles. What was Aunt Maxina saying? She began to read aloud. "Oscar Ortega, who came from the Guadharra, arrived north of the Great Forest about two-hundred fifty years ago. He lived amongst the Mayza tribe, and over a period of time, became one of them. While they taught him the ways of the tribe, Oscar taught them about his god, Kammbi."

"What does that have to do with our family?"

Aunt Maxina lifted her eyes from the book and stared at me with the look I'd seen over years at the dinner table. It demanded I remain quiet.

"Oscar became close to a young woman named Adrianna. She was fascinated by him and became his companion for many years. A short time after becoming his companion, Adrianna was pregnant. He was shocked and horrified by her pregnancy. Oscar revealed to her that his wife, Sophia, who lived back in Guadharra, would have to know about their tryst. And he would have to return to his homeland to tell her," she continued.

"Where did you get this fiction from?" I said incredulously.

She didn't look up from the book. "Oscar told Adrianna he had committed an act of *passha,* and he had to seek reconciliation with both his wife and Kammbi. While he returned to his homeland, Adrianna gave birth to a boy on the fourth day in the month of Beru. She named him Charles."

"Are you saying that this Book of Kammbi tells the real origin of Charles?"

"Yes," she answered and closed the book.

I stood up and began pacing the room. "Are you telling me that Sidney Azur is not Charles' father? This man from the north, Oscar Ortega, is his father. How did you come to believe this? How did this Book of Kammbi get here?"

"Sit down, my nephew," she said and reached for my hand. "I knew you would have a lot of questions. Remember what you said in the park. You said we must stick with truth. And now I'm honoring that request."

I stopped pacing after that comment. She had a point. If this was the truth, what kind of freedom would it mean for the family, the city, and me?

"Diondray, I have always suspected that Charles's origin and background were different than what I heard growing up. My father, your Great-Uncle Myro, hinted to me and Olivia that our history was more complicated than was ever spoken about around the family home."

"My mother knew about this too."

Aunt Maxina nodded. "So does Xavier. But they refuse to believe it. Charles and Mother Adrianna are sacred to them, and there's no room for any other interpretation."

"So if this is true, what does my reading have to do with it?"

"I wasn't finished yet, my nephew."

She turned her eyes back to the book. "Oscar returned from his homeland with his wife, Sophia," Aunt Maxina continued. "She forgave his act of passha but demanded that Adrianna and the baby leave the Mayza tribe. The elders agreed with Sophia.

"At least two thirty-day cycles had passed when Adrianna and Charles left the tribe and made it through the Great Forest. They arrived at the Kammara Sea with the help of the leopard, Reuel. Adrianna and Charles were famished and worn out from that voyage. They were rescued by members of the Makala tribe. Sidney Azur, the leader of the tribe, took the woman and the child as his own."

I got up from sitting and pulled the shawl closer to my body. It felt like I was inside of a freezer. Ama's Faddar's air-conditioning worked very well.

"Oscar Ortega is Charles's father? Then why did he allow Adrianna to be banished from that tribe?" I started pacing.

"To answer your first question, yes. To answer your second question, I believe his act of passha was the reason," she answered and looked up from the book at me.

"What is an act of passha?"

"First, stop pacing. Your energy level is too frenetic and out of balance with your life chart."

I didn't want to stop. I was listening to an alternate history I had never heard before and trying to wrap my mind around the possibility that it could be true. If so, why would my family hide this history?

"Please, my nephew, sit. You were born under the sign of the Water Bearer and can be open to new information and change."

I stopped pacing and remarked, "Change! What does being born under the Water Bearer have to do with *this?* You just read from some old book I've never heard of that Charles, our founder and the orakl of orakis, has a different father than we believed. The life chart has nothing to do with that!"

Aunt Maxina smiled and grabbed my hand. She pressed to pull me down. I wanted to break her grip but realized she was risking quite a bit in telling me this history. I relaxed under her grip and sat down.

She returned to reading. "Oscar Ortega was devastated by the banishment of Adrianna and Charles from the tribe. He prayed to Kammbi for reconciliation with her and his son. Kammbi refused his request because of his act of passha with her. There had to be consequences for that action.

"However, Oscar's repentance allowed another way to be established for reconciliation. Oscar wrote these words that he heard from the Eternal Comforter: 'Because of your obedience in leaving your homeland to come to a new land, I will continue to make your name great. Even though you have lost a child due to your act of passha, you will have a descendant who will unite the entire land. And the people will believe that Kammbi is the Lord of all. Those who always believed in me and those who didn't believe in me will create a new people, establishing peace and sanctification throughout this land.'"

Aunt Maxina stopped reading and closed the book. "Diondray, I believe you are that descendant."

Chapter 4

"What if everything you believed can now be questioned? What if everything you have been taught might be a lie? What if the truth you believed is not the truth at all?" I asked the audience.

It had been five days since I was with Aunt Maxina at Ama's Faddar. What she read to me from the Book of Kammbi had been on my mind ever since. I had to get my thoughts into a themily and read it to the people here at Aliki Park.

The month of Carm had arrived, and the heat had subsided somewhat, hopefully in anticipation of the rain we usually received during this time. We needed it. It had not rained since the middle part of the month of Nayur, the first month of the year.

I took my mind off the potential for rain and scanned the faces of the audience. I was not sure if I should reveal the information I had heard from Aunt Maxina. I didn't know how they would handle it. Would they believe totally, like she did? Would they reject it, like my mother and Uncle Xavier had? Or could they think there was some truth to it like I did?

"What are you talking about, Mr. Azur?"

I searched for where that comment came from. I saw it was my critic from the last reading. Instead of being in his usual spot, he was a few rows farther back. I guessed he hadn't made it to the park early enough to get his spot. However, his bald head stood out amongst the blow-out hairstyles around him.

"How do you handle it when what you have been taught proves not to be the truth?" I continued. "Do you confront the one who has told you lies? Or do you continue to believe in the lie you have been taught all your life?"

"Mr. Azur, you have to confront the one who has told you the lies," someone else answered.

I looked for where that voice was coming from. It was a woman wearing an orange plaid shirt, who stood next to my critic. It didn't appear they were together as a couple.

"I remember what you read last time," she said. "The truth is freedom. You must pursue freedom. If you don't, Mr. Azur, who will?"

The audience nodded in agreement. I knew I could not turn away from everything I had heard in the last few days. I had to pursue the truth and find out why this history of Charles, Mother Adrianna, and Oscar Ortega was never discussed at all.

* * *

Trayvonne and his newest lady friend, Sialia, came to visit me at my place later that evening. Sialia looked like a carbon copy of Portia. The only difference between the two women was Sialia's height. She stood about six feet tall, and it surprised me that Trayvonne would go after a woman taller than him. When he squeezed her ample behind before they sat down on my sofa, I knew why he had overlooked her height.

"Bro, I must say that was the first time I saw the audience look out of sorts after a reading," he said as I handed him a glass of mango juice.

"You noticed it too," I replied and gave Sialia a glass of mango juice as well.

"They could sense something was troubling you," Sialia added.

"Everything I have ever believed could be a lie."

I explained to them about my meeting with Aunt Maxina at Ama's Faddar. The Book of Kammbi had been in Charlesville all these years, and no one in my family had ever discussed it. Our history as a city and a family was different than I had ever heard of—and our future might be different than I'd ever imagined.

Trayvonne stared at me in shock, and Sialia shook her head in disbelief.

"My grandfather was right all these years," Trayvonne said softly. "Ama, he was right."

"Right about what?" I asked.

"My grandfather used to tell me stories that Charles Azur was not a blood member of the Makala tribe. He and Mother Adrianna came from the north, And that Sidney Azur was not his real father. I thought he was just making it up."

"This is getting beyond belief," Sialia interjected.

"My grandfather said there was a book that would reveal the true history of how this city came to be. Bro, you know that he is not a descendant of the original Makalas."

I nodded and remembered Trayvonne telling me about his grandfather. How my family had pushed the descendants of the original Makala tribe out of the city.

"We must go visit him," he said.

* * *

It took three days for Trayvonne to get the visit set up with his grandfather. I spent that time pondering whether I was truly a descendant of Oscar Ortega. I thought about him wanting to reconnect with Charles. Even though he had committed this act of passha, why wouldn't his god, Kammbi, let him seek reconciliation with his son?

If someone makes a mistake and seeks to correct it, shouldn't they be forgiven? I wondered. *Does that mean I shouldn't seek forgiveness for any mistakes I've made in my life?*

Questions like these ran through my mind constantly. Aunt Maxina had placed the Book of Kammbi back into the room in Ama's Faddar after our visit. I would like to have read the whole thing to see what forgiveness meant to Kammbi.

Trayvonne came to pick me up for the visit in his RKV-100. The RKV-100 was not built anymore and was considered a rare automobile. Trayvonne kept that car looking like he had just bought it from the automobile dealer. It was the envy of the neighborhood. He sped away from my home, awakening my neighbors.

A few minutes later, he reached Ama's Parkway, going northeast through the west side, heading toward the center of the city. I saw the vacant buildings and hated how my family had neglected this area of our city.

"Are you all right, bro?" Trayvonne asked.

"Oh, just looking at the scenery."

"Remember, your Uncle Xavier doesn't care about the ants."

"Well, he should care, Trayvonne! What have these people done to him? Whether they came from Terrance during the migration or are native-born to the city, they deserve to have this area looking just like the east side."

Trayvonne laughed and replied, "You really do hate your uncle."

I must admit, at that moment I probably did. Maybe he felt the same way about me. We had never gotten along with each other, and I had stayed away from him while I was living in the family home. Things only seemed worse now that I had moved out.

Trayvonne made a left off Ama's Parkway onto Charlesville Highway, heading west out of the city. He turned on the stereo, and Ruben Davar began to play. He was considered one of the greatest

Kammarice musicians in all of the cities south of the Great Forest. Kammarice music originated from the city of Terrance and Ruben Davar cut his teeth amongst best in that city. Ruben had played in the other cities of the region: Walter's Grove and Adrian. He was the first non-singer to play for my family when Uncle Xavier took over as ruler from Great-Uncle Myro. His sound on the guitar had been describing as enchanting. Hearing his music on the stereo calmed me down.

Twenty minutes later, we were outside of the city limits and reached an area where the remaining descendants of the original Makala tribe lived. Uncle Xavier forced them out of the city and they settled here, where they could live together and keep honoring those traditions.

The Makala lived in small, red-mud homes bunched together, much like their ancestors had lived during Charles and Mother Adrianna's time. It made me realize how much the city had changed, and it saddened me as well. It meant our past was gone except here, and the city had lost something because of it.

"I bet you haven't come out this far before," Trayvonne said as he parked in front of the first house of the village.

"No, I haven't. We have definitely gone back in time."

He laughed as we both got out of the car.

The home was faded red and had one big window that looked like two eyes fused together. Trayvonne knocked and opened the door. I followed him inside. The living room was sparsely furnished, with one long sofa and a huge life chart hanging on the wall behind it. I had never seen one that size before.

"Hello, Trayvonne and Diondray," an old man said as he entered the living room, holding a tray of mango bread and a couple of glasses of mango juice.

I was surprised he knew my name. I assumed that Trayvonne had been talking about me to him quite a bit.

"I knew you were coming to see me, grandson. We had an overcast day out here, and that was a sign to be expecting visitors."

"Scarro, I brought Diondray to you to talk about Charles," Trayvonne said as we both sat down on the sofa.

Scarro sat on the ground in front of us. He had earned his name. Scarro had a face-long scar that started underneath his left eye and went across his plump cheek, then ended where his left jawbone and neck met. I wondered what had happened to him.

"Charles Azur's father was not Sidney Azur, the great leader of our tribe." he started. "His father came from the north and tried to teach his strange beliefs to the Makalas."

"I heard that recently, Scarro," I replied.

He faced me and said, "I bet it surprised you, being an Azur."

I nodded and replied, "Why would my family hide this history?"

"A woman's scorn can last a long time," he replied and laughed softly. That laugh had a tone like he had dealt directly with a woman's scorn. "Mother Adrianna was banished by her tribe because she had a child with Oscar Ortega. She loved him and wanted to stay amongst her people, even though Oscar was married.

"The elders decided to have her and the baby, Charles, leave the tribe. Their tribe had become a believer in Oscar's god, Kammbi, and knew this was the only choice they could make under the circumstances."

"Oscar's wife, Sophia, came to that tribe, and Adrianna had to go," I replied.

Scarro laughed softly again and said, "At least for a young man, you have some understanding about women. That will serve you well when you are ready to find a mate."

I glanced at Trayvonne and saw his smirk. It had been several years since my last lady friend, Mara. That had ended, and not well, when I decided to go live on the west side.

"I heard that read from the Book of Kammbi," I said.

Scarro had a surprised look on his face. "The Book of Kammbi is still here in Charlesville?"

"Yes, it is in Ama's Faddar. My Aunt Maxina read it to me recently."

"Scarro, I didn't believe it when Diondray told me. I remembered you telling me the stories about that book being destroyed after Oscar came to reconcile with Charles," Trayvonne added.

"Yes, my grandson. I did tell you that. And if the Book of Kammbi is still here . . . then Oscar's words will be fulfilled after all."

"His words?" I asked.

"Diondray, I'm sure your aunt read Oscar's words—his prophecy. That there will be someone to follow after him and unite this land as one. He couldn't reconcile with Charles because his god wouldn't allow it. However, Kammbi granted him a wish, and that prophecy was it."

I couldn't believe what I was hearing. He knew about Oscar's prophecy! I was starting to believe in this alternate history.

* * *

Mother was surprised when I called to ask if I could come and visit with her. She told me that after the birthday dinner, she had thought it would be a while before she saw me again. Two days had passed since my visit with Scarro and Trayvonne, and I needed to hear from Mother about all I had learned.

Willar greeted me when I arrived and took me immediately to Mother's wing of the family home. Uncle Xavier, Aunt Maxina, and Mother each had a separate wing, and for the most part, each one stayed in his or her own area until social gatherings or official family business. He knocked and opened Mother's room door.

"My son, so good to see you," she said as we embraced.

I released her quickly as Willar closed the door. How much did he know about this other history? If he knew, was my family forcing him to be silent?

"Is there something wrong?" she asked as we both sat on chairs next to her dresser.

Mother's room had that signature smell from her favorite perfume, a mixture of mangoes, brownberries, and oranges. She was dressed in a long, flowing orange dress that made the whole room feel tropical.

"Mother, who is Oscar Ortega?" I said.

She frowned. "Where did you get that name from?"

"Was he Charles's birth father?"

"Where did you get that blasphemy from? Answer me! You are still my child!"

"I thought Charles Azur's father was Sidney Azur, our great ancestor. His father was actually a man from the north, Oscar Ortega. This man had an inappropriate relationship with Mother Adrianna that caused her to be banished from her tribe. How long have you known this history?"

She reached for my hands. "Lies! Who has fed my son these lies? It is time for you to return back home and get away from those west siders and their stories."

I got up from the chair. "Why has this never been mentioned in the city's official records or at the festivals?"

She stood from her chair and grabbed me. I felt the sting of her slap landing on my left cheek.

"Don't you ever talk about this history with me or anyone else! Sidney Azur took care of Mother Adrianna and Charles as his own. He's a real man, not that man from the north."

"So it's true," I replied and pulled out from her grasp.

"I will find out who told you this information, and they will be punished for it. You better not spread this history amongst those ants on the west side."

"Too late for that. I guess this is what it means for the truth to set you free."

"You will never be forgiven if you spread this history, my son."

"Well, at least I won't be known as a liar."

"Get out!" she screamed.

I searched Mother's face and sensed a cold spirit from her that I had never known existed. I left the room.

Chapter 5

It had been almost a full month since I had given my last themily reading. We reached the end of Carm, and rain had not come. Hopefully Lir, the fourth of the year, would bring much-needed rain to the city.

Trayvonne had called me several times in the last few days. He knew my schedule of giving a reading every seven to eight days and had not seen me at the park since the beginning of the month. He was concerned.

I assured him that I would be okay. I had a lot to digest and couldn't get my words right for my next themily. He accepted that excuse and vowed to check on me until I returned to Aliki Park.

I was trying to decide if I should reveal more of this alternate history. Mother had been wrong when she said the people on the west side told lies and false stories about our family. They believed the history of Charles and Mother Adrianna just like the east siders did. It was what we all learned at school. I worried they would have a strong reaction like Mother had, and that kept me from giving my readings on schedule.

Finally, I returned to the park. I stood on the podium and noticed the look of anticipation on their faces. I glanced to my left and saw Trayvonne and Sialia giving me smiles for encouragement. I must admit I was surprised that he'd kept Sialia for this long. Trayvonne must finally have found the right woman for him.

At that moment, I wished Mara could be here. I would have liked a companion to be here for support, someone with whom I could share how I really felt about everything I had learned in the last couple of months. But Mara felt like Uncle Xavier and Mother about the west siders. They were not on her level, and she didn't want to associate with them.

"I said in my last reading, 'Do you confront the one who has told you the lies? Or do you continue to believe in the lie you have been taught all of your life?'"

The audience was silent.

"I got a response from someone in the audience that you should confront the one who has told you the lie. *And that truth is freedom,*" I said and glanced at Sialia. "Well, I have confronted the person who has told me the lies. It was my mother."

The audience shook their heads, mouths agape in disbelief.

"I have found out some history in our family that has never been told before."

I paused and scanned the audience. They remained silent, but their faces disagreed with my claim against Mother. Even though my family did not treat these people well, they felt some loyalty toward them. I took a couple of deep breaths and started pacing on the podium.

"Charles' father is not Sidney Azur, the great leader of the Makala tribe." I continued.

"That's crazy, Diondray!" someone from audience shouted at me.

"Everyone knows that Sidney Azur is Charles' father and Mother Adrianna was his wife," another audience member shouted.

I raised my hand to quiet them and continued. "Let me finish before you make a judgment on my words."

The audience obeyed my request and let me continue with the reading.

"That last statement has been confirmed by a book that has been in our city since Charles was alive. My aunt, Maxina Azur, read it to me at Ama's Faddar in the month of Beru. It is called the Book of Kammbi."

"The Book of Kammbi! I thought that book was gotten rid of during Charles's time," someone from the audience yelled out.

I didn't look out at the audience to find out where that comment came from. Instead I continued to pace the podium. "I believed that as well. However, the Book of Kammbi is still here in Charlesville, and it reveals that Charles's father was a man from the north named Oscar Ortega."

"He can't stay still on the podium!" another voice from the audience yelled back. "He's making this up!"

"Who made you get up to say these words, Mr. Azur?"

The audience erupted, and I had lost control of them. Trayvonne and Sialia rushed to join me on the podium. She reached out for my arms and stopped me from pacing.

"It's all right," Sialia whispered in my ear while embracing me. "You did good."

Trayvonne was calming down the audience by telling them my claim was true. I looked out and saw the audience split into two sections. They were some CRG guards coming toward us.

The CRG guards were the city's police force and protectors of our family. All of them were at least 6'3 inches tall and weighed close to 230 pounds. The guardsmen wore their custom bright yellow shirts and shorts that glowed off their night-colored skin. They demanded respect, and no one attempted to cross them.

"Diondray Azur, please come with us," the first CRG guard who reached the podium said.

"For what?"

"You are being taken into holding for disseminating false information to our citizens," he replied.

"What false information?" I replied as I was being escorted away.

He didn't reply as the rest of the CRG Guards opened a path through the audience. I overheard some of the audience's comments that thought I should be arrested. Was this the kind of freedom that truth brought?

* * *

I arrived at a holding cell a few minutes later. I was told that Trayvonne and Sialia had been interrogated at the park and allowed to go home. It was disheartening to see that some of the audience wanted the CRG guards to arrest me. I'd thought I had gained their trust after the past three years of themily reading. Now I realized that trust could be fleeting, especially after revealing a truth that could change so much.

I demanded an explanation as to why I was brought to the holding cell. I had not done anything wrong, and I wanted to know who made the decision to keep me here. I was told I would get an explanation from the head of the CRG soon.

The size of the holding cell reminded me of my storage room back at the family home. I kept my wardrobe and shoes in that storage room, and it was not a large space. The bare walls of the holding cell were aqua blue like the water in the Bay of Charlesville. A long table similar to the one in Scarro's home took up the center of the holding cell. I sat on the bench next to the table and wondered how long I was going to be kept here.

A few minutes later, I heard a turning at the door of the holding cell. A guard entered, holding a tray of food and a pitcher. He looked young, probably about my age of twenty-three. I didn't know they allowed those of my age to join them.

The guard placed the food tray and pitcher on the table. There were brownberries, cooked redfish, and bread on that tray. I looked into the pitcher beside the food and saw it was brownberry juice. I guessed those who were held in this cell didn't get mango bread and mango juice. That was not good.

Moments later, he returned with a glass and placed it next to the pitcher. He left the holding cell without talking. At least I was going to get fed while being here.

After dinner, the head of the CRG came to visit me.

"Mr. Azur, I know you have questions about this arrangement," he said as he sat down at the table. "But I'm only allowed to say that you will be held indefinitely until your family decides to release you."

"Indefinitely! Who decided that?"

"Mr. Azur, you are being accused of spreading false information to our citizens. And that is considered a crime. However, you belong to the first family of the city and can't be punished like someone else under the circumstances."

"A crime!" I said and rose from the table. "I'm considered a criminal for speaking words? Who authorized this arrangement?"

The head guard rose from the table and stood in his official position. His hands were by his side and his posture straight as a line.

"You can relax," I said and sat back down.

He complied. "Your mother, Olivia, has made this accusation against you. She believed you were going to spread information about the city's history that was untrue."

"My mother!"

He nodded and continued. "We will make sure you have the best living arrangements for as long as you are here."

He left. I couldn't believe Mother would have me arrested and brought here. Why was she so passionate about keeping this alternate history from being revealed to our citizens?

* * *

I was treated well in the holding cell for the past three days. The bed was quite comfortable for sleeping, and I had three meals each day. The guardsmen were pleasant under the circumstances. However, none of that helped the fact that Mother had placed me here.

I was told that Mother was coming to visit today. My emotions ranged from anger to sadness in anticipation of her visit. What kind of explanation would she give me for my predicament? I didn't want to see her, and I thought about asking the head guard not to allow her into this cell.

I heard the doorknob turn, and Mother entering the cell. Her face was swollen from tears and had a horrified look. It didn't comfort me.

"My son, I'm so sorry," she said with her arms open wide for an embrace.

I didn't move from my seat at the table. "Have I become a criminal to you?"

She sat down across from me. "It was Xavier, not me. I would never have my child placed in a cell like this. These are for the ants you have decided to live amongst."

"So the head guard lied to me?" I said with anger rising in my voice.

"He didn't lie, he's just wrong. I told Xavier about our last conversation, and he got angry with you. He wanted to teach you a lesson. I thought he would demand you return home. I never thought he would have you placed here—and then blame it on me."

"Why would you tell him about our conversation?"

"My son, you know that Charles and Mother Adrianna have been held in high regard for our entire history. Their place in our city is sacred and can't be changed."

"How I do know that? I don't understand why you never taught me about this other history. Why hide it?"

The tears streamed across her cheeks. "You don't understand! And you are the sign of the Water Bearer, and that makes you an agent of change. If you begin to believe in that history . . ." she said and placed her hands over her mouth.

"What does my sign from the life chart have to do with this?"

Mother rose from the table. "My son, I beg of you, please don't believe in what you have been told."

"Get me out of here."

"I can't," she said as she started to leave. "Only Xavier can decide that."

"What? He's your brother and has put me here for no good reason. You and I both know you control a lot of what happens in this city. Have him get me out of here, Mother."

"I can't . . . my son," she replied and left the cell.

I banged my hand on the table in frustration. Why didn't she want to believe in this alternate history? What did the life chart have to do with it? How long would Uncle Xavier keep me here?

* * *

Seven days passed after Mother's visit, and I grew weary of being in the holding cell. I asked the first guardsman who brought me lunch and dinner about any contact from my family. He said there was nothing to report. Uncle Xavier had decided to punish me for what I'd read at Aliki Park—with arrest, imprisonment, *and* the silent treatment. I missed standing at the podium doing my themily readings. I liked looking at the audience's faces for their reaction. I missed hanging out with Trayvonne as well.

At this point, I was still unsure about who put me here: Mother or Uncle Xavier. I could believe it was Uncle Xavier more than Mother. However, I remembered the way she had looked at me when I was in her room. The coldness I'd felt from her revealed something deeper in Mother's personality that I didn't know existed. She was willing to protect the history of Charles and Mother Adrianna even at the cost of her own child.

And what did my sign as a Water Bearer have to do with it? She knew I never fully believed in that stuff. That was from the old culture. No one on the west side followed their life charts; the immigration from Terrance had affected local beliefs too strongly. Those immigrants believed in multiple gods and I heard about the one named Megaro, that came from Kammara Sea.

Those old beliefs had become a conversation piece at parties or other social events. You would say, "I'm a sign of the Porpoise," meaning you were born in the month of Carm, the third month; or "I'm a sign of the Ox," meaning you were born in the month of Aym, the fifth month; or "I'm a sign of the Stingray," meaning you were born in the month of Veme, the eleventh month. No one attached any real meaning to it. But the east siders, including mother and Uncle Xavier, held on to those old beliefs.

The cell door opened, and the head guard entered the cell. He placed paper and a pencil on the table in front of me.

"You are not supposed to have this," he said tersely. "However, I've heard about your themilies from some of those folks at Aliki Park. I think you deserve to keep working on them."

"Thanks."

He gave a slight smile. "You are welcome. I'm sure you have a lot of frustration and need a release."

I laughed as he left the cell. It felt good to finally laugh.

* * *

I prefer clarity over agreement. I prefer disagreement rather than blindly accepting history or what I have been taught as truth. I prefer discussion amongst those I disagree with over punishing others because they differ with me.

Those were the first words I wrote in the holding cell. Simple as they were, it took several hours for them to come out. The head guard was correct—I needed a release.

I worked for several more hours on the themily. It was about having clarity and how the memory of the past can be altered from what really happened. What other history had my family kept away from the people? I was starting to question everything I had been taught as a child.

I heard the cell open, and I looked up from writing.

"Hello, my nephew," Aunt Maxina said with a troubled look on her face. "It's time to leave."

"Leave?"

"Xavier may be the ruler of this city. But I'm his sister, and my nephew should never have been locked into a holding cell like a criminal."

"How?"

"Don't worry about that, my nephew. Gather your things, and let's get out of here. Time is limited."

I grabbed my paper and writing instrument and followed her out of the cell. I didn't know how she got Uncle Xavier to release me. But I was glad she had.

"Thank you, Aunt Maxina," I said as we walked out the building. I glanced at the guard who guarded my cell and could see the shocked look on his face. He didn't believe I was supposed to leave that holding cell so soon.

"I have something to tell you, my nephew," she said as we reached the automobile that was parked in front of the building.

I searched her face and noticed that same troubled look from earlier.

"You will have to leave Charlesville."

"Leave Charlesville?"

"Xavier doesn't know I got you out," Aunt Maxina continued. She clasped my hands. "I've tried every means possible to get you out of there. Xavier was born under the sign of the Ox and is extremely stubborn. He wanted to keep you in that cell until you apologized to him for mentioning that history to those people at the park."

Aunt Maxina's eyes watered while she was talking. This was the first time I'd ever seen her show emotion.

"I knew I had to get you out. Even if it means jeopardizing my own future."

She placed my hands on her cheeks, where I felt her tears. I felt closer to Aunt Maxina at that moment than at any other time I could remember.

"This automobile will take you to the airport. There is a flight to Santa Sophia waiting for you. I don't know if I will ever see you again, my nephew. But I want you to know I love you like my own son, and your words spoken at the park are finally coming true. Truth is freedom."

She released my hands and opened the automobile's door. "There's something inside you will need for your journey. "

I got inside the automobile and closed the door. I looked to my left, and on the seat beside me was the Book of Kammbi.

Chapter 6

The driver for the automobile Aunt Maxina had arranged for me whisked through the streets of the west side in order to get to the airport as quickly as possible. I found out his name was Keevah, and he had been a friend of Aunt Maxina for many years. I didn't know she had a friend who was a driver and could help her in a situation like this. Apparently, unlike my mother, Aunt Maxina would form relationships with "the help."

I asked him about Santa Sophia. He knew nothing about the city other than where my flight was going to take me. Since I could only see the back of his blow-out hair, I wondered if he knew the danger of helping me escape Charlesville.

What will I do in that city? How am I going to live? Did Aunt Maxina arrange for me to be taken care of? My mind raced with questions.

I grabbed the Book of Kammbi that was lying on the seat beside me. A piece of paper fell out it. I pulled the paper close to me. It read:

My nephew, I know you have a lot of questions at this moment. You are leaving home and wondering why. You will get the answer to that question when you arrive in Santa Sophia. I have some instructions for you. Please follow them.

First, you will need to read the Book of Kammbi on your flight to Santa Sophia. You will need to learn about Oscar Ortega and what he did for this land. His story is covered in the Baramesa section of the Book of Kammbi. Baramesa means "promise," and there are seven books in that section.

Second, you must go to the kahall of Santa Sophia when you arrive. You will meet with someone there who will take care of your living arrangements. You will not have to worry about how you are going to live.

Third, I want you to know that I will be all right even if Xavier finds out that I helped you escape Charlesville. I believe you are the one who will unite this land as one, and the Great Forest will not be a barrier between us anymore. However, you must be accepted as one of their own. Their approval of you will be critical if you are to fulfill Oscar's prophecy.

I love you, my nephew. Truth is freedom.

I folded the paper and placed it back into the Book of Kammbi. Aunt Maxina had embraced this alternate history and the beliefs of this book. I hadn't known there was a connection between Santa Sophia and Charlesville. If I fulfilled Oscar's prophecy, would the people of our city become believers in Kammbi?

* * *

Keevah opened the automobile door once we arrived at the airport. I noticed he had a suitcase in his left hand.

"Good luck, and may Ama be with you," he said and handed me the suitcase.

I grabbed the suitcase and opened it to place the Book of Kammbi inside. The automobile's door closed, and it dawned on me that I was leaving Charlesville. Keevah drove away, and I walked into the airport.

A CRG guard greeted me after I entered the building. He had a stern look on his face, and his thick eyebrows accentuated his displeasure.

"Follow me, Mr. Azur," he said sharply.

I obeyed his instruction and, moments later, reached the boarding area for my flight.

"May Ama be with you," the guard said and left the boarding area.

I watched him walk away and wondered what kind of trouble he would be in when Uncle Xavier found out he had helped me leave the city. Aunt Maxina must have planned my departure days ago in order to get a driver, a guard, and a flight for me. Who knew she could wield that kind of power?

"Hello, bro."

I turned around in surprise and saw Trayvonne with his reassuring smile. He had a new woman with him as well.

"I'm here to see you off," he told me.

"Aunt Maxina told you about this arrangement?"

"Yes, she planned this while you were in the holding cell," he replied. "She's a believer in that Book of Kammbi."

"She is indeed," I replied.

We shook hands and embraced. He was my only real friend, and I would miss him a lot.

"Before you go, I want you to meet Anissa. I told her everything about you and this arrangement."

Anissa smiled and replied, "Nice to meet you finally. May Ama be with you."

I nodded. Trayvonne, I realized, would never settle down with one woman. He had first choice of all the women on the west side and could get rid of this latest one once he got bored with her and have a new one the next day. Anissa was short and voluptuous, as he liked them, but had light-green eyes that contrasted nicely with her caramel-colored complexion. She was the prettiest woman I had seen him with so far.

"Truth brings freedom, bro."

"It does, Trayvonne."

We shook hands and embraced. I knew that was the last time I would see my best friend.

* * *

As I settled into my seat, I realized I was the only passenger on the airplane. I remembered when I traveled to the cities of Terrance and Walter's Grove as a kid. Flying on the plane delighted me then and made me want to be a pilot after each flight.

However, I did not have those feelings as I prepared to leave Charlesville.

A woman wearing a yellow blouse and green shorts approached me from the front of the airplane.

"Mr. Azur," she said.

"Yes."

"I'm Stayssia, your flight assistant for this trip to Santa Sophia. The flight will take about four hours. Once we are safely in the air, I will bring your meal. Sit back and enjoy the flight." She smiled and turned back toward the front of the airplane.

I opened my suitcase and pulled out the Book of Kammbi. I had to follow Aunt Maxina's instructions. I hoped I would understand what I read and that the belief system in this book—the belief system of the lands north of the Great Forest, where I was heading—would make some kind of sense to me.

"All systems have been checked, and we ready are for takeoff," a voice said. It sounded like it came from through a stereo speaker. It must have been the pilot.

Good-bye, Charlesville. Will I ever return to you?

* * *

A few minutes after liftoff, I started reading the Book of Kammbi. It was divided into two sections: Ryianza (meaning "covenant") and Baramesa (meaning "promise"). There were seven chapters in each section. The Ryianza chapters covered the origin and life of Kammbi, while the Baramesa chapters covered the origin and life of Oscar Ortega.

I saw a folded corner on one of the pages at the beginning of the Baramesa section. Aunt Maxina must have used that folded corner as a page maker for herself. Or was it for me?

The first two chapters described how Oscar Ortega left his homeland in Guadharra in order to follow Kammbi's command. He received a vision one morning before going to work. Then a voice said, "Oscar Ortega, I have chosen you to establish a new land that will worship and honor me. You must leave everything behind in order to do it."

Oscar didn't know where that voice came from. But it spoke to him each morning for seven days until he agreed to follow its command. I wondered if his family, especially his wife, thought Oscar had gone mad when he told them about that voice and what he had to do.

However, the Book of Kammbi didn't record that conversation between Oscar and Sophia or his other family members. The first chapter ended with him leaving Guadharra with only a single bag of clothes. It seemed to me that Kammbi wanted his followers to obey him without question. Also, that they must trust him completely.

The second chapter recorded the journey from Guadharra to the Ortega Hills. A couple of items stood out for me. The journey took fifty days where he crossed the Omarra Sea, and Oscar learned about something called "the Eternal Comforter." I didn't totally understand what the Eternal Comforter was. It seemed that when Oscar confessed his belief in Kammbi, he received the Eternal

Comforter as a gift. Was it a spirit? Another god?

The other item that stood out to me was when Oscar reached the Great Forest. He was traveling through the forest, being guided by the Eternal Comforter, when trouble came. A couple of huge black cats surrounded Oscar. They were getting ready to pounce on him when a brown-spotted leopard jumped onto one of those black cats, knocking it away from Oscar in the nick of time. The other black cat continued toward its prey, but a strong wind lifted it away from him.

After that ordeal, the brown-spotted cat returned to Oscar. At first, he thought the cat wanted to attack him too. However, Oscar realized the leopard was friendly, and he saw the bruises it had received in the fight with the first black cat.

The leopard approached Oscar and lifted his head to show a shiny tag around its neck. Oscar read the tag and learned the leopard's name Reuel. *Reuel* meant friendship, and from that day they were inseparable.

"Your aunt told me this was your favorite meal," Stayssia said, interrupting my reading.

I looked up. She had brought mango bread, bluefish, and mango juice. Bless Aunt Maxina. I didn't know what they ate in the north, but I could guess this would be the last time I ate my favorite meal.

"Enjoy," she said and walked away.

I sure would. I hoped that Santa Sophia would have food as good as this meal.

After I ate, Stayssia came back to take my plate and clean the tray. She said we would be landing in two hours and that the pilot would make an announcement as the plane made its descent into the city.

Two hours until I reached my new home. I still had an uneasy feeling in my stomach, but the reality of my situation was starting to take hold. I pondered whether Oscar Ortega had the same kind of feelings when he left Guadharra. Or did he totally trust in Kammbi?

I returned to reading the Book of Kammbi. Chapter 3 was the

shortest in the Baramesa so far. It highlighted Oscar's expedition into the cities north of the Great Forest: Santa Teresa, Alicia, and Issabella. The next three chapters would go into greater detail about his expedition into each those of the cities.

The last chapter in the Baramesa grabbed my attention. It was Oscar's trip to Charlesville. He attempted to reconcile with Charles, but he already knew that Kammbi wouldn't allow it because of his act of passha with Mother Adrianna.

> *Oscar Ortega was devastated by the banishment of Adrianna and Charles from the tribe. He prayed to Kammbi for reconciliation with her and his son. Kammbi refused his request for reconciliation because of his act of passha with her. There had to be consequences for that action.*
>
> *However, Oscar's repentance allowed another way to be established for reconciliation by Kammbi. Oscar wrote these words that he heard from the Eternal Comforter: "Because of your obedience in leaving your homeland to come to a new land, I will continue to make your name great. Even though you have lost a child due to your act of passha, you will have a descendant who will unite the entire land. And the people will believe that Kammbi is the Lord of all. Those who have always believed in me and those who didn't believe in me will create a new people, establishing peace and sanctification throughout this land."*

Those were the words Aunt Maxina had read to me in Ama's Faddar. Seeing them on the page brought Oscar's prophecy to life. I wondered if the prophecy was the real reason this history had been hidden in our city all these years? Did my family fear becoming believers in Kammbi?

I was still having trouble understanding the act of passha and its consequences as well. Kammbi took this act of passha seriously, but from what I had read, I couldn't get a reason why. I couldn't help think that Kammbi wanted perfect followers and would punish them for any mistake they made. Did I even want to follow a god like that?

I knew I would have to get a better understanding about the act of passha if I was going to fulfill Oscar's prophecy.

"We are beginning to make our descent into Santa Sophia," the pilot announced over the intercom. "Diondray, please make sure you are secure in your seat belt. We will be landing shortly."

I took a deep breath and finished reading.

Chapter 7

The airplane landed safely in Santa Sophia. The flight didn't feel like four hours, since I was reading the Book of Kammbi most of the way. However, I was ready to stand up and walk around a bit.

"Diondray, I hope you find what are you looking for in Santa Sophia," Stayssia said as she approached me.

"I do as well."

Stayssia smiled and replied, "I don't know why Maxina wanted you to come here. I wish your stay to be a short one and that you return home very soon."

She embraced me, and it seemed like she knew I would not be returning to Charlesville anytime soon. I released myself from her embrace, knowing that Santa Sophia would be my new home.

* * *

I received my suitcase when I got out of the airplane, and then I walked into the airport. It was enormous. Glass windows were everywhere, and the walkway had red and green squares that created an intricate pattern. The lighting was so bright I momentarily put my hands over my eyes. I guessed the people of Santa Sophia liked bright colors and lights.

I saw a sign for the bus and walked in that direction. I exited the airport. An oversized, bright orange bus was parked in front of it. I had never seen an automobile that huge before. It was the size of three RKV-100s and could seat at least twenty-five people.

"Going to the kahall?" the driver yelled as he opened the door to the bus.

"Yes, how did you know?"

"I was told be here at this time," he said. He got up from his seat and exited the bus. "There was a flight coming from a city south of the Great Forest, and only one passenger would be arriving."

I nodded as he grabbed my suitcase.

"Plus, I could tell you are from a city south of the Great Forest. No one dresses like that here in Santa Sophia."

He laughed as I followed him onto the bus. He placed my suitcase in the first seat behind him on the right side of the vehicle. I sat down in the seat next to it.

"They don't wear shorts in Santa Sophia?"

"No! Mister?"

"Azur. Diondray."

"No, Diondray Azur," he replied and continued laughing. He had a deep laugh that came from his stomach. "You would freeze to death if you wore clothes like that all the time. I hope you have some long pants and long-sleeved shirts."

He closed the automobile's door and drove away from the airport. I hoped Aunt Maxina had provided me with some clothes that I could wear here.

"What city are you from?" the driver asked.

"Charlesville.

"Charlesville . . . hmm, I remember seeing your city on a map in school."

"A map?"

"Yes. You don't have maps in Charlesville?"

"No, I'm afraid not."

He laughed again and turned around to face me. "No maps in those cities south of the Great Forest? That's surprising. I hope you didn't grow up in a city that was behind the times."

The driver returned to his driving position and focused back on the road. Was Charlesville really "behind the times," as he put it? I hoped this would not keep me from being accepted by the people of this city.

"What is your city like?" the driver asked.

"Well . . ."

"Horacio."

"Horacio, Charlesville is my home, and the only place I've known. So it would be easy to tell you all the wonderful things about it. Like the food, the beach, and that I can wear shorts all year long."

Horacio chuckled and interjected, "Those shorts-wearing days are over."

He made a right turn, and I looked out the window to catch a view of the city. I noticed there were no people walking on the streets. Where was everyone?

"Do people come outside?" I asked.

"This is the beginning of the month of Lir. From now until the twenty-first day in the month of Aym, the people remain inside until the evening. We are honoring Oscar Ortega's journey from Guadharra to the Ortega Hills. "

"The journey took fifty days."

Horacio turned around with a surprised look on his face. "Yes, it did! How did you know?"

"I've been reading the Book of Kammbi."

"Did you get a copy at the airport?"

"No, I have a copy with me."

Horacio turned quickly back to the road, but he sounded very interested. "There was a copy of the Book of Kammbi in Charlesville?"

I nodded. Horacio was looking at me through the big mirror above him.

"I don't know if I can believe that."

"The Book of Kammbi was left there by Oscar Ortega. How else would I have a copy?" I began to open my suitcase. I pulled out the book and held it up for Horacio to see.

"Great Kammbi!" he replied, still looking at me through the mirror.

I saw the eyes raised in disbelief.

He started to slow down the bus and pulled over off the road. "I have to see it."

Horacio stopped the vehicle and got out of his seat. I finally noticed his small stature. Horacio was about half of my height. However, he had oversized hands and broad shoulders that made up for his lack of size. Horacio's most prominent feature was his thick mustache and beard that covered the bottom of his face.

I handed him the Book of Kammbi, and the surprised look on his face revealed all I needed to know. If the people of Santa Sophia didn't believe that Oscar had left the Book of Kammbi in Charlesville, then gaining acceptance here would not be an easy process. As I wasn't different enough, I was all carrying an object that would be controversial.

Horacio stared at the Book of Kammbi for several minutes before returning to driving. I thought we were going to have further conservation, but he remained quiet until we reached the kahall of Santa Sophia. That worried me too.

"Here's the kahall of Santa Sophia," he said after parking. "May Kammbi be with you."

Horacio got up and grabbed my suitcase. He had a distant look on his face. "Do you know what this means, Diondray?" he said and grasped my shoulders with those oversized hands. His grip was strong.

"What does it mean?"

"Oscar's prophecy may finally come true," he replied. He shook my hand. "Go to the newcomer's assistance area."

I nodded in acknowledgement.

* * *

I followed the main sidewalk to the entrance of the kahall. Overhead was the kahall's reddish-orange, dome-shaped roof. The rays of the sun reflected off of it. I could only look at that roof for a few seconds before I had to lower my eyes.

I reached the main entrance, where I heard a slow creaking sound as the door pulled back for me to enter.

"Welcome to the kahall," a man wearing a white shawl said. "Service is not for a couple of days. How can I help you?"

The man's smile was wide, stretching his mouth back toward his cheeks. His teeth were so white they appeared painted like a kid would do in a coloring book.

"I'm looking for newcomer's assistance?" I asked.

"Newcomer's assistance. Are you from another kahall?"

"I just arrived from Charlesville. I'm Diondray Azur."

The man seemed startled by my comment. "Charlesville . . . you said?"

"Yes. It's south of the Great Forest. Have you heard of it?"

"I have heard your city mentioned before, Diondray," he replied. "Follow me."

The man led the way further into the kahall and turned right after a few steps that led to another hallway. It was dark inside. There were little flames of light encased in cylindrical cases every few steps. And there was music playing softly as well. I didn't know where it came from.

"I have been told that someone would arrive here today, unexpectedly. I was to have a room ready for that person. I believe I just found out whom that person is," the man said as he stopped at a door on the right side of the hallway. He opened the door and continued, "You can rest here for the evening. I will bring you dinner later."

"I'm going to stay here?" I asked.

"I will find out before evening has ended," he replied. If that's the case, I'm Second Esperah Leo Carranza. May your stay in Santa Sophia be welcoming."

He left the room.

* * *

The room was spacious. The bed occupied the left side of the room and had a red blanket covering it. Opposite the bed was a long, rectangular window and a desk underneath. The wall between the bed and the window had a painting of a man floating in the air. There was a white glow surrounding him and the words, *He's always with us.*

I dropped my suitcase next to the desk and walked over to the painting. I touched it, and it felt rough, like a shell rock on the beach. I looked at the man, at his bearded face and large eyes. I felt like he was staring back at me. I knew it was Kammbi.

There was a knock on the door. I turned around, and Second Esperah Carranza came into the room.

"Dinner," he said and placed the plate on the desk. "I don't know what you eat in Charlesville. But I hope this meal will be similar to what you've had."

"Thank you."

Second Esperah Carranza stood back from the desk with his fingers intertwined on his chin. "Kammbi, may you bless this meal that Diondray will eat, and may you give him guidance while he's here in Santa Sophia," he said softly.

I sat down. On my plate were fish, a bunch of red circular things with long stems, and a green leaf of some type. It didn't look that much different from what I ate back home.

"I've heard the people south of the Great Forest love fish and fruit. Well, we don't eat a lot of fish here in Santa Sophia, but I was able to get this for you. The fish we do eat comes from the city of Alicia. Hopefully, the fish and cherries will remind of your city."

"I will let you know how it tastes."

He smiled at me and turned to leave the room. "I will return in a while to collect the plate. Enjoy."

I ate the fish first. It had a flaky texture that I could easily chew. Its aroma was not as strong as the bluefish I regularly ate. I wondered if the fisherman or whoever had cooked this meal was able to wash out the fishy smell somehow. Overall, it was very good. I was relieved to know there was at least one food item I could eat here in Santa Sophia.

I tried the red fruit with the long stem. I spit it out after a couple of bites. The fruit was not sweet like a mango, and my teeth bit into a seed. I bit into the green leaf and found it tasted like paper. I needed flavor in my food, and I would never eat this green leaf again.

Second Esperah Carranza returned to the room a couple of hours later. He was still dressed in his shawl and carried a lamp in his right hand. "You didn't eat much of the cherries and the verde lettuce," he said after placing the lamp next to the desk.

"Not for me. But I love the fish."

He grabbed the plate and said, "I'm glad at least the fish was enjoyable for you. I will return in the morning for breakfast, and after that you will get to meet Diakono Copperwith. I've been told that this room was set-up for you. You will live here while you are in Santa Sophia."

Second Esperah Carranza intertwined his hands again and bowed before he left the room. He was as formal as the CRG guards who patrolled back home. Did he ever relax outside of his duties? Or did Kammbi expect people like him to act that way all the time? I decided I would like to talk to him and find out more about his duties here at the kahall Also, they knew I was supposed to arrive here like Aunt Maxina mentioned in the letter. How long had this arrangement been planned?

It was time for my first night of sleep outside of Charlesville. Tomorrow would be a new day and a chance to get a better idea of how I was going to fulfill Oscar's prophecy.

* * *

I woke up to the sun's glare in the room. I got dressed and walked over to the desk. I had placed pencil, paper, and the Book of Kammbi on the desk before I went to bed. I was looking forward to writing my first themily here in Santa Sophia.

Second Esperah Carranza came into the room with breakfast a few minutes later. He was carrying a plate in his right hand. I could see a thin, circular white piece of bread covering the entire plate. There were sliced cherries, corn, and strips of meat mixed together on top of the bread. I had never seen that combination of foods mixed together before—but it didn't look bad. The meal's presentation was colorful and interesting.

"I thought you should try one of main dishes here in Santa Sophia for your next meal," Second Esperah Carranza said as he placed the plate on the desk.

"What is it?"

"A changa," he answered. "One of our favorite foods here."

Second Esperah Carranza smiled and waited for me to try it. The aroma from the plate opened up my nostrils, and I picked up the plate from the desk.

"Roll the edges of the bread over the ingredients and lift it off the plate."

I followed his instruction and took a bite. It was delicious. The tartness of the cherries balanced out the textures of the corn and strips of meat.

"I knew you would like it. Changas are mostly eaten for breakfast here in Santa Sophia."

I nodded as I took a bigger bite of the changa.

"Is that the Book of Kammbi?" he asked.

"Yes, it is," I replied after swallowing my latest bite. "It came with me from Charlesville."

"Oh my!"

"This copy of the Book of Kammbi has been in my city since Oscar's expedition when he attempted to reconcile with his son, Charles. I just found out about that a couple months back when my Aunt Maxina showed me where it had been all these years." I put the changa down on the desk as I spoke.

Second Esperah Carranza stared at the Book of Kammbi like was going to put a hole through it. "May I touch it?" he asked in a soft voice.

"Sure," I said and handed him the book.

He didn't grab it but touched the cover with his fingers. "Oh, my! Diakono Copperwith was right all this time. He believed there was a copy of the Book of Kammbi south of Great Forest."

"I don't understand. I just read in the Book of Kammbi that Oscar came south of the Great Forest to reconcile with Charles. It says he left a copy of the Book of Kammbi before returning back here. You have copies of the book here and read it, don't you? Do the people of Santa Sophia not believe those words written?"

Second Esperah Carranza removed his fingers from the Book of Kammbi. I clutched the book in my hand to keep it from falling to the floor.

"Unfortunately, not all do." He lowered his eyes after that comment and intertwined his fingers.

"Do the people of Santa Sophia truly believe in Oscar's prophecy?"

"Not a lot of us, Diondray. Maybe you are truly here to change that."

Chapter 8

Second Esperah Carranza led me out of the newcomer's assistance area and back through the main entrance of the kahall. The lights were still on even though it was daylight. Did they ever burn out? We reached outside and turned left on a sidewalk that took us around the east side of the kahall.

"Diakono Copperwith's office is a little walk from here. Good thing it's a nice day outside. The heat from the months of Yul and Gus are still some time away," he commented.

"It's hot in Charlesville all year round."

"I could tell by what you are wearing, Diondray. I hope you have some longer clothes in your suitcase."

"I stand out by wearing shorts."

Second Esperah Carranza looked back at me and gave a small smile. "Yes."

It was the first time I had seen him smile. This was a chance to get to know him better. Trayvonne would tell me never trust a person who didn't smile. That meant they were always thinking and living inside their head. It was not good for anyone to live like that, and it could make you go crazy if you did it long enough.

We reached another building adjacent to the main entrance of the kahall. Second Esperah Carranza opened the door and was greeted by a tall man with blond hair and a dimpled chin. I felt his presence as soon as I came into the office. Second Esperah Carranza intertwined his fingers and bowed before the tall man.

"Diakono Copperwith, this is Diondray Azur of Charlesville."

"Welcome, Diondray," Diakono Copperwith said as walked up to me.

His presence made me take a step back. However, he grabbed my shoulders and pulled me into an embrace.

"I believe we have our second person from south of the Great Forest here at kahall of Santa Sophia, Second Esperah Carranza," he continued and released me from his embrace.

"Second person from south of the Great Forest? Has someone else come before me?"

There was a long black sofa against the wall on the left side of the room. Diakono Copperwith motioned for me to sit. He sat on the opposite end. Second Esperah Carranza stood solemnly upright next to the door of Diakono Copperwith's office.

"I imagine you have a lot of questions and wonder if you are really the one to fulfill Oscar's prophecy," Diakono Copperwith said.

At least he got right to the point. "Yes, I do," I replied.

"Before I attempt answer your questions, let me explain who am I and my role. Also, I will explain Second Esperah Carranza's role as well. It's important for you to understand how things work here."

Diakono Malcolm Copperwith spent the next couple of hours explaining his and Second Esperah Carranza's role here at the kahall. The role of diakono was a highly regarded one. Diakonos were the elder members of the kahall and ran its business and administrative functions. The morrim, head of the kahall, chose diakonos in a detailed and thorough manner. Each kahall had at least three diakonos but no more than seven. The kahall of Santa Sophia had four, and each one had his specific function in the building.

Diakono Copperwith's role was that of teaching and education. He was second-in-command behind the morrim and filled in for him at various times, teaching the kahall service for the entire congregation.

Second Esperah Carranza's role was considered the entry-level position in the kahall's organizational structure. Second esperahs were basically there to assist the diakonos and provide whatever they needed. He was one of twelve second esperahs at the kahall of Santa Sophia and one of three second esperahs assigned to Diakono Copperwith.

After that explanation, I got a better understanding of each man's role and had a sense of why Second Esperah Carranza was so formal. I realized I could never do his job. I knew I could not wait at beck and call for whatever the diakonos needed.

"Second Esperah Carranza, could you get lunch prepared for us?" Diakono Copperwith asked at that point.

Second Esperah Carranza bowed and replied, "Right away, Diakono Copperwith." He left the office.

"He serves you well," I said.

Diakono Copperwith stared at me briefly. I felt his eyes looking right through me. I hoped I hadn't said something wrong.

"A second esperah's role is to be a servant. One can't be a leader without being a servant. Kammbi is our greatest example of this."

"Does Second Esperah Carranza ever get to voice his opinion?"

Diakono Copperwith smiled. "I see why you left your family's home and got out from under Xavier's rule."

"How did you know about that?"

"Why do you think you are here, Diondray?"

"Aunt Maxina. You know her?"

Diakono Copperwith rose from his seat and continued. "Yes. I met your Aunt Maxina during the month of Carm. She was convinced you are the one to fulfill Oscar's prophecy. She flew up here to Santa Sophia in advance of you coming to pave the way."

I couldn't believe what I was hearing. Aunt Maxina had set this up all along! How long had she believed in Kammbi and kept it a secret from the family?

"When I heard her story, by the guidance of the Eternal Comforter I knew it was true. You are indeed the one who fulfill the prophecy. She asked to me to take care of you. That's why you are here in Santa Sophia."

I spent the rest of the afternoon with Diakono Copperwith. We had lunch and talked about each other's history. He knew that I wrote themilies and that it was my readings that convinced Aunt Maxina of my true role. Diakono Copperwith said that when Aunt Maxina came here, he didn't want to believe her. However, when she started telling him the history of Oscar Ortega coming south of the Great Forest and that he had left a copy of the Book of Kammbi in Charlesville, Diakono Copperwith knew she was telling the truth. He began to prepare then for me coming to Santa Sophia.

I asked Diakono Copperwith if Aunt Maxina had told him how long she had believed in Kammbi. He answered by saying she became a convert after she arrived in Santa Sophia. Before then, Aunt Maxina believed our city's official history was false, but she could never pursue that belief because of the repercussions she would have faced from Uncle Xavier. I wondered how someone could have changed their beliefs so quickly. Could we really believe in anything for a long time? Or would we all change when we were persuaded to do so?

I would return to his office tomorrow, and he would give me a tour of the city. He wanted me to bring the Book of Kammbi. Diakono Copperwith had to see it for himself. If I had the very book Oscar Ortega had left behind, like Aunt Maxina told him, then I would have the oldest copy of the Book of Kammbi in existence.

* * *

I returned to Diakono Copperwith's office the next morning, the tenth day in the month of Lir. I wore my first pair of pants below my knees. Aunt Maxina had packed them in my suitcase. It felt like tape or some kind of gift-wrapping around my legs. The pants were uncomfortable when I started walking but got better when I arrived at the diakono's office.

I held the Book of Kammbi in my left hand. Diakono Copperwith rose from his seat behind the desk to greet me. We embraced, and I rested the Book of Kammbi underneath his shoulder blade.

"Is that it?" he asked.

I nodded after we released one another and handed the Book of Kammbi to him.

His eyes opened wide, and a big smile came over his face. Diakono Copperwith looked like a child receiving a present for his birthday celebration.

"Oh Kammbi," he said softly and caressed the cover. "All these years, and Oscar really had left this book south of the Great Forest. They have had it all this time."

"Yes," I replied.

He opened the book, and I heard the flipping of the brittle pages. I didn't know how long the book would last now that it was out in the public.

"The morrim has to see this," he said and handed the Book of Kammbi back to me.

"Does the morrim believe in Oscar's prophecy?"

Diakono Copperwith's childlike smile left his face immediately, and a distant look came across his face. "Yes, as a teacher of our beliefs. But in his own heart, I truly do not know."

"Why is that?"

The diakono sighed and replied, "It's much too involved to get into a detailed discussion about it. There are a lot of people here in

Santa Sophia who believe Oscar should never have gone south of the Great Forest to try to reconcile with Charles. Since his dalliance with Charles's mother was his greatest act of passha, he should have accepted his punishment from Kammbi and not tried to have a relationship with his out-of-wedlock son."

"What's wrong with a father wanting to have a relationship with his son?"

"I hear the anger in your voice, Diondray," he said and sat down on the sofa. "And I agree with you. But the believers and followers of Kammbi take passha very seriously, and having a child with a woman you're not wedded to is one of the greatest acts of passha a man can commit."

"So does Kammbi allow for forgiveness?" I asked and joined him on the sofa.

"He does, Diondray. But Oscar Ortega is considered one of the greatest men who ever believed and followed Kammbi. And many of us still feel ashamed about the act of passha he committed. We do not want to believe he could do such a thing."

"So then why would Kammbi create this prophecy for him? He could have stopped Oscar from coming south of the Great Forest."

Diakono finally smiled and said, "Kammbi had to honor his word. I've been told you have read the Book of Kammbi. I don't know if you have read the Ryianza yet. Book 6 is where Kammbi talks about when a person commits an act of pasha. They must ask for *aphemmia* in repayment for that transgression."

"Aphemmia?"

"Forgiveness. Repentance, demonstrated through action," he continued. "We will all commit acts of passha during our lives, Diondray. No one is perfect but Kammbi. And through him we can ask for aphemmia. If it is truly from the heart, it will be granted to us like it was for Oscar Ortega."

Oscar Ortega had been granted aphemmia in order for him to try to reconcile with Charles. However, he did not mend the relationship between him and his son. So did Kammbi really give forgiveness to Oscar Ortega? I thought when forgiveness was granted, the past had been wiped away. I wasn't sure about this act of aphemmia concept.

* * *

"I guess the people of Santa Sophia must like big automobiles," I said as we arrived at Diakono Copperwith's car.

He smiled as he unlocked the doors. "It's a Carranza 125 LC. One of the biggest cars we have still in production. However, this model is ten years old, and the newer versions are much smaller."

"We don't have automobiles this big in Charlesville. The RKV-418 is our largest automobile, and is about half the size of this one."

"My wife has the best automobile in the family. This one gets me from one part of the city to the next part."

"I assume you are telling me that when I get married, I should give my wife the best automobile."

Diakono Copperwith laughed as he drove away from the kahall. "You are a perceptive young man, Diondray Azur."

It was good to hear him laugh, especially after our conversation about the act of aphemmia. I was still troubled by their concept of forgiveness. I didn't understand how a God could grant forgiveness but still allow the punishment from the mistake they made. I knew I would have to get a better understanding of this concept before Oscar's prophecy could be fulfilled. If I couldn't even understand or accept this basic part of their faith, I certainly couldn't be the one to unite the lands around belief in Kammbi!

"We are traveling on Oscar Ortega Boulevard," Diakono Copperwith announced. "The road starts at the kahall of Santa Sophia and travels north through the center of the city. Then it turns northwest, going into the Ortega Hills."

"The Ortega Hills. Is that where Oscar first settled when he arrived in this land?"

"Correct, Diondray. Oscar settled amongst the Mayza tribe at that time. They lived in those hills and believed they were sacred. The tribe worshipped the hills like they were a god."

"Oscar changed that with his belief in Kammbi."

"Yes, he did. The elders of the tribe knew immediately that Oscar Ortega was a special man, and they embraced the teachings about Kammbi shortly after they met."

"How could they just easily reject their own beliefs like that?" I asked as I looked out onto Oscar Ortega Boulevard. There was no one outside walking the streets.

"When the truth is presented to you, either you accept or reject it."

"You accept or reject it? How do you know if it's really the truth?"

The diakono smiled. "You are a questioner, and I know you have struggled with the beliefs you grew up with."

"Yes," I answered as he turned into a parking lot.

"You're at the age where you are questioning everything you have been taught. Questions are good and should be asked. But acceptance and trust in something bigger than yourself is the next step for you, Diondray."

Diakono Copperwith parked the car. He made it sound so easy—but I didn't think it was. How could I trust and accept so easily when I had just found out a history that had been deliberately hidden from the people of Charlesville and myself for many years? That kind of deception would make you question everything you ever believed in. Hadn't the believers and followers ever questioned Kammbi or even Oscar Ortega? Had Diakono Copperwith ever questioned his beliefs? It seemed the morrim had.

* * *

"This is the first stop on our tour of Santa Sophia," Diakono Copperwith said as we walked across the street from the parking lot. We crossed a wide, triangular street and headed toward a statue that was some distance away. "On each side of us are the marketplaces of Sophia, I and II. The marketplaces are the main shopping areas for the center of the city. They have been around since the last years of Oscar Ortega's life."

On either side of us, the marketplaces were long, rectangular buildings of a sandy color that made them indistinguishable from everything else in this area. There was no one walking into them or out from them, so I would not have noticed them if Diakono Copperwith hadn't told me about them. "We are in the marperia," he continued. "There is the area where many people come from all over the city to relax from shopping at the marketplaces, eat their food, or people-watch. As you know, there is nobody out in the daytime during the period between the Festival of First Cherries and the upcoming Festival of Sinquinta."

"The Festival of First Cherries was on the first day of Lir?" I asked. I could smell the yellow flowers that were in bloom as I walked through the marperia. This place had a serenity that held the busyness of the city at bay.

"Yes, it is. As you read in the Book of Kammbi, the Festival of First Cherries celebrates the sacrifice Kammbi made for humanity. The squeezing of the first harvested cherries represents the blood he sacrificed for our acts of passha. The cherry juice poured on the ground represents Kammbi's blood covering those acts of passha and washing them away for good."

We reached the statue. It towered over the marperia. The statue of Kammbi was cloud-white and stood straight up with arms extended wide. It appeared he was welcoming everyone to come to him. The face and beard were similar to the painting in my room back at the kahall.

I shifted my eyes to Diakono Copperwith as he bowed down in front of the statue. I heard mumbling from him but couldn't make out what he was saying. It lasted several minutes before he returned to standing.

"Diondray, this is the statue of Kammbi. It is one of the most sacred artifacts of the city. Oscar Ortega had this built in the last year of his life. The elders of the Mayza tribe wanted to build a statue of Oscar for everything he had done. However, Oscar wouldn't agree to that, and he asked that the statue be built in the image of Kammbi instead. It is the most visited attraction in all the cities north of the Great Forest."

I heard the excitement in his voice. The statue was a beautiful piece of artwork, and I could imagine what it meant to him.

"Excuse me, young man. Where are you from?" a voice said behind me.

Surprised, I turned around and saw an elderly woman with a determined look on her face. She had long wrinkles underneath her eyes and squinted in order to look at me.

"Hello, Lady Patricia," Diakono Copperwith interjected. He gently took her left hand to help her balance.

"Thank you for your assistance, Diakono Copperwith. However, this young man is not from here, and he has not answered my question."

She released herself from the diakono's grip and placed both her hands on my face. They were rough against my cheeks, and I wanted to pull my face away. But the elderly woman's gaze kept me in place.

"I'm from Charlesville. South of the Great Forest."

She nodded and smiled, revealing that a few of her teeth were missing on the bottom. "I knew you were from south of the Great Forest. I saw you and Diakono Copperwith crossing the street, and I had to find out who you were. You have a presence about you, and I know you are here in our city for a reason."

Diakono Copperwith gave a surprised look at the elderly woman and said, "Diondray, Lady Patricia Carranza is one of our longtime parishioners in the kahall, and her family is one of the original families of the city. She comes to Kammbi's statue often, even during this time between the festivals."

"Diakono Copperwith, this young man will learn about me and my family soon enough. Can you stand next to me in front of the statue?"

Lady Patricia reached out her left hand for me to hold it. I grasped her hand and honored her request. Diakono Copperwith stood on the opposite side of her.

She released my grip and bent down in front of the statue. "Young man, please join me."

I did.

Lady Patricia grabbed my hand and bowed her head.

"To the One who blesses us all, please hear my words. I saw this young man a short time ago and knew instantly there was something special about him. I believe you brought him to our city for a reason that is not known to me. However, I would ask you to guide him. To ease his mind and help him to understand that what he thought of as the truth is no longer true. Please show him what the truth is and what you want him to do. Lastly, I ask that you teach him to learn to trust you. Because he will need your trust from this point forward."

She opened her eyes and looked over at me. "May Kammbi bless you. Diakono Copperwith, give him your wisdom and guidance into trusting the One who deserves all of our trust."

Diakono Copperwith nodded in agreement as he helped Lady Patricia to her feet. She walked away from the statue, and I stared after her, wondering what had just happened.

Chapter 9

I had now been in Santa Sophia for fourteen days, and it dawned on me how fast time passes, waiting for no one. I spent two days thinking about Lady Patricia. I wanted to talk to Diakono Copperwith about her and that prayer. But he had been busy with teaching and fulfilling his role while the morrim was away. I could have asked Second Esperah Carranza about Lady Patricia—from their last names I suspected they were related—but I did not know if I could ask him personal questions yet.

I decided to pull out my pencil and paper to write a themily. I placed those items on the desk and gathered my thoughts on what to write. I hadn't written a themily since being here. I needed to put words to paper.

> *People can sense a connection with you immediately. People can sense if you are genuine even if they don't know you. But how can they sense if you are meant to do something special? Who can give people that ability?*

A sense of relief came over me after getting those words down. My had mind raced until I wrote the questions out, and doing so brought me an ease I needed. Was the Eternal Comforter inside of

Lady Patricia the same way he—or it—was inside Oscar Ortega? I had read in Books 3 through 6 of the Baramesa that the Eternal Comforter played a significant role in helping Oscar during his travels. I assumed from that reading that all believers and followers of Kammbi had the Eternal Comforter inside of them. If so, how could a spirit live inside of you?

My sense of relief dissipated after these additional questions popped up in my mind. I returned to writing before Second Esperah Carranza brought breakfast.

* * *

I met with Diakono Copperwith a couple of hours later. He was ready to take me on the next part of the city tour. As we headed for the car, he told me about his time leading service and some of his duties while the morrim was out. I could tell that he really enjoyed teaching the congregation and did not like the administrative responsibilities. He wanted me to attend the kahall service when he taught again in about ten days.

"The Elissa Quadrant is the most prominent quadrant of our city," Diakono Copperwith started to explain. "We have four: Elissa, Niomi, Noa, and Enoshe."

"Oscar Ortega's children," I interjected.

The diakono nodded and continued, "Elissa was Oscar's eldest child and like him in personality and temperament."

After we passed the marketplaces of Sophia and the marperia, Diakono Copperwith made a left turn off of Oscar Ortega Boulevard and onto Elissa Drive as the signpost read. I looked out the window to see no one was out during the daylight. He explained that the reddish-orange rectangular buildings on both sides of the street were businesses that had closed because of the festivals. The buildings were all the same height, and there was no trash on the sidewalk. I had never seen a city street this clean before, not even on the east side near my family home.

"Elissa Drive is the second longest street in the city behind Oscar Ortega Boulevard and the only other street that goes up into the Ortega Hills. I grew up hearing the story that Elissa wanted this road to go up into the hills so it could join up with her father's road and they would always be connected."

"Was she Oscar's favorite child?"

Diakono Copperwith gave me a sharp look. "She was indeed. Those two were a lot alike, even though they clashed when Elissa came of age. But he still favored her over the other children."

"So Oscar had conflict in his family as well."

"Yes, Diondray, he did. That really affected his relationship with his boys, Noa and Enoshe."

"I read in Book 7 of the Baramesa about Elissa and Niomi. Not a lot about his sons. Is there a reason for that?"

"Some morrims before my time believed Oscar was ashamed of his sons and how they behaved, so much so that he didn't want the scribes at the Konseho of Kammbi to write about them. I don't know if I believe in that theory, because Oscar spoke fondly of Noa and Enoshe before he died. After his experience with Charles south of the Great Forest, I think Oscar realized he had to love his sons even more.

"The Konseho of Kammbi?" I interjected.

"The Konseho of Kammbi is a council that governs all the cities north of the Great Forest. Everything we do on a citywide level goes through them. If you are the one who will fulfill Oscar's Prophecy, then we will have to meet in the city of Issabella."

The road curved, and Diakono Copperwith became silent. I noticed the homes in this quadrant were the same color as the businesses we had passed earlier. Did anyone in this quadrant have a home of a different color? If they did, would the other residents be angry? Would the morrim or diakonos get mad? What about Kammbi? It seemed this god was big on conformity. In that way, he was like Ama. Was that just something about gods—that they wanted their believers and followers to act the same and be just alike?

"Are you noticing something that needs an explanation?" Diakono Copperwith asked.

"The homes are all the same color, and the street is clean. Charlesville doesn't look like this."

He laughed and replied, "It is because we are in the Elissa Quadrant, and it is home to the governor, the city council, and the three original families of the city."

"So this area gets special treatment?"

"Of course, Diondray," the diakono replied. "Doesn't your family get special treatment as the ruling family of Charlesville?"

I nodded reluctantly.

"Are you uncomfortable with that status?"

"Yes, I am. Because I've seen how those with special status treat those who are beneath them. It's not pleasant."

"Your Aunt Maxina was right. At least I know you will not be fascinated with the riches and prestige of this and the Niomi Quadrant."

Diakono made a right turn, and I could see the Ortega Hills like they were right in front of us. I must admit I wanted him to stop the automobile so I could stare at them. They were reddish-orange like the city but carved like an artist creating fine work with a tool. I had to believe that Oscar Ortega was taken by these hills when he first arrived in this area. While Charlesville was flat and surrounded by water, these hills were the complete opposite of that landscape. I knew right then that I would have to spend some time here.

"On to the Niomi Quadrant," Diakono Copperwith announced.

* * *

About ten minutes later, we arrived in the Niomi Quadrant. The main road here was the Niomi Trail. Diakono Copperwith explained the road started from the western edge of the quadrant and curved to the south, where it met with Oscar Ortega Boulevard.

Businesses lined both sides of the street, stacked together like the blocks I had played with as a kid. There were tall buildings right beside short ones, and I imagined jumping from one to the next. I didn't see any homes here. Diakono Copperwith told me this was the business area of the city. The Niomi Quadrant created the wealth for the city, and most of the people worked here.

"I will have to bring you back to this quadrant after the Festival of Sinquinta," Diakono Copperwith said, "so you can see the busyness of Santa Sophia when everyone is going to and from their jobs."

'I didn't know you could make buildings that tall," I replied and pointed to the tallest building I had ever seen in the distance. It had to be taller than Ama's Faddar or any other building back home in Charlesville. I wondered what kind or business or operation resided in that building.

"That's the Carranza Tower, the tallest building in all of the cities north of the Great Forest," Diakono Copperwith answered. "It was built about thirty years ago as a tribute to Diego Carranza, the city's first magnate."

"He came to this area after Oscar Ortega returned from Guadharra to get his wife, Sophia."

"Correct. From Book 3 of the Baramesa. Diego wanted to find his own way as a man. Oscar agreed to allow Diego to return with him to this area on one condition."

"He had to become a believer and follower in Kammbi."

"Yes, he did. And Oscar would not stop him from becoming the magnate he desperately wanted to be."

"Diakono Copperwith, it seems to me that Kammbi wants everyone to conform to a certain way in order to become a believer and follower of him. Does he accept any believer and follower as who they truly are?"

Diakono Copperwith smiled and replied, "Doesn't Ama want his believers to conform to their life charts? All gods have a standard of how they want their believers and followers to be. The real question is which god's teachings and standards are right and can truly apply to all people, whether you believe and follow him or not."

I frowned. "We don't have a free will?"

"We have a free will, Diondray. You can choose to believe and follow in Kammbi or not."

I didn't expect that answer. "So there are some people here in Santa Sophia who don't believe in Kammbi?"

"Yes, there are. We will see them in the Noa Quadrant."

I sat back in my seat, surprised. I had thought everyone here in Santa Sophia believed in Kammbi. Maybe there wasn't total conformity here after all.

"You also have a free will to choose whom you will marry, what occupation you will obtain, and many other lifestyle choices as well. However, if you truly want to do something significant, then you must be guided by something outside of your will and abilities."

"For you and the people here, it's Kammbi."

"For you, it's Ama and the life charts."

"Who is right?"

"I believe you being here, Diondray, has answered that question."

* * *

I spent the next couple of days with Second Esperah Carranza. I got a complete tour of the kahall of Santa Sophia, and he began to explain

73

a good portion of its history. I learned that the Mayza tribe built the kahall in Year 5 A.O.A. (After Oscar Arrived). Oscar wanted a place built where people could gather to honor Kammbi and meet to learn his teachings. He felt it was important for the believers and followers to get together on a consistent basis in order to stay connected and strengthen their belief in Kammbi.

In the beginning, the kahall only had a meeting room for the congregation and a kitchen to serve everyone after the teaching service. Over the years, the kahall of Santa Sophia added more land and built housing for the morrim and the diakonos, a school, offices for the employees, and the newcomer's assistance area to help the citizens of Santa Sophia and visitors like me.

It was the largest kahall in the city and held the most prestige as well. All the other kahalls in Santa Sophia looked to this one for direction and guidance in how to teach and lead their people.

I could hear the pride in Second Esperah's voice when he explained the history of the Kahall. He seemed to be really proud that he belonged and worked at such a place.

After the tour and before Second Esperah Carranza left for the evening, I asked, "Why do you believe in Kammbi so strongly?"

He stopped before he reached the door and turned to face me. "Because I trust him," he replied.

"How can you trust a god who wants you to conform to what he wants? That isn't trust to me. It's conformity."

His expression changed. "Diondray, you believe that true freedom is becoming your own man. However, true freedom is trusting in something bigger than yourself."

"How can you trust in something that will not let you be yourself?"

"Do you think I'm not being myself?" he asked.

I nodded. "I have seen you wear the same clothes every day since

I've arrived here. You bring breakfast, lunch, and dinner at the same time every day. And our conversation, other than right now, has been all about your duties. I thought by now I would get to know more about you."

"You never asked, Diondray. Also, by serving you, I'm doing everything I am supposed to do."

"Don't you want to break free from all this duty?"

"No. I have no reason to do so. Being a Second Esperah has been everything I've ever wanted, and Kammbi has blessed me greatly." He grabbed the doorknob but searched my face as he formulated what to say next. "Believing in Kammbi has shown me the difference between who I am and what I am."

Second Esperah Carranza exited my room.

After he left for the evening, I sat at the desk and pondered over his last comment. Was there a difference between who I was and what I was? Weren't they one in the same? How did you know if they were different?

I wrote those questions on the paper, and it got me started on a new themily. He had given me the words I needed to write, and I knew exactly how I wanted to place them on the paper.

Who am I? What am I?

I would never have thought there was a difference between those two questions. Have you ever thought of about it? Maybe learning how to answer those questions will cause you to truly grow up. For most of my life, I believed who I was meant belonging to the most prominent and ruling family of Charlesville. And I believed what I was meant the same. Now, I realize that what I am has always been different than who am I. And I'm here to find out what am I.

I stopped writing and looked at those words. At that moment, I thought about Aunt Maxina and wished I could share this with her. Also, that I could have read this at Aliki Park. I would have loved to see the reaction of the audience.

* * *

"We will head to the Enoshe Quadrant for the next part of our tour," Diakono Copperwith said as we drove away from the kahall. "What you saw in the Elissa and Niomi Quadrants was very different from what you will see here."

The sun had gone down and dusk had arrived. For the first time I saw people walking on the sidewalk as we drove by, and there were other cars on the street as well. It was a welcome sight.

"Is there a reason you wanted to take me to the Enoshe Quadrant in the evening?" I asked.

Diakono Copperwith looked over at me and replied, "I was allowed by the Morrim of the Kahall to take you out in the evening. I thought you would want to see the actual citizens of Santa Sophia asked for permission. I'm pretty sure you were beginning to think that this period between the festivals was a little much."

I chuckled and said, "It's different. How much longer before people can come out during the daytime?"

I saw the street sign, Enoshe Way, as Diakono Copperwith made a right turn off Oscar Ortega Boulevard. People were walking leisurely along the street, and I wondered where they were going.

"There are still thirty-three more days before the twenty-first day of Aym."

"Thirty-three more days until they can come out during the day? How can people abide this way every year?"

"Ritual for some. Tradition for some. But for me, as a diakono, it is a matter of trust and obedience."

"Obedience!"

"I know that's going to be hard for you, Diondray."

I stayed quiet. He was right.

"You just said that the Enoshe Quadrant is different than the previous quadrants I've visited," I asked in order to change the subject. "Why is that?"

As Diakono Copperwith drove further on Enoshe Way, I saw people starting at the automobile as we passed by. I didn't know if they were surprised to see a diakono in this quadrant or if they were looking at me and saying to themselves, *Who is this person? He's not from here.*

"What you saw in the Elissa and Niomi Quadrants was the city at its best. You will see the opposite in our trip today."

"How does Santa Sophia treat those who are less fortunate?"

"I wouldn't call them less fortunate, Diondray. Wealthy or poor, they all belong to Kammbi. However, there's always a division between those who have a lot and those who don't. And the quadrants reflect that division."

"That's one of the big differences I had with my family. Uncle Xavier believed that the east side should always be kept up and promoted as the face of Charlesville. He thought the west side should only be given the basic necessities to survive, and then the people could fend for themselves. That's not fair."

"I would agree with you about that not being fair. But humankind has always divided itself between those who have and those who don't. The question becomes, what do *you* do with the resources you have?"

I turned away from looking out of the window and faced the diakono. "Are you saying that those who don't have should just accept their position in life? They shouldn't have the same resources as those who are wealthy?"

"It's not that simple, Diondray. Even if you give everybody who is poor the same resources as those who are wealthy, it will not matter unless they accept who they are. There are a lot of people who believe that equality of resources means equality of social status. But it doesn't. People will always divide into their own social status groups because of what they believe about themselves, and they will always want to be around people who are like them as well."

"But what's wrong with giving everyone the same amount of resources? It just doesn't seem fair that some people have a lot and others don't."

"Again, you are stuck on the words *fair* and *equal*. Many people, even those here in Santa Sophia who believe and follow Kammbi, feel the same way you do. But if they would read the entire Book of Kammbi, they would know that Kammbi has never taught about fairness and equality of resources. He teaches only that no matter what your social status is, you must trust in him to guide and provide for you. He understands that we will always be resentful and envious of those we believe have a higher social status than ourselves. And when you are resentful or envious, then you have committed an act of passha. So it always returns to who you really are and what are you becoming."

I tried to puzzle my way through the diakono's answers. He kept coming back to the idea that we should accept our social status and place our trust in a god who would give us everything we needed. But how could we be sure that a god would do exactly as he promised? I had seen those on the east side get special treatment from the oraki in order to get their wishes granted by Ama. It seemed that those who had got what they wanted from Ama, but those who didn't have were expected to follow their life charts without question or deviation. So how could I be sure that this god, Kammbi, would not do the same thing as Ama?

"This is Kahall Thirty-Seven," he said as he parked in front of a kahall. It was white, small, and nondescript. I thought maybe it was some kind of historical place that he wanted me to see on our tour. Also, I wondered why he didn't believe in the fairness and equality of resources for all people. If those of us who had lots of resources gave up some of them to those who didn't have, wouldn't that create a better society?

"It is the kahall I grew up in."

"Smaller than the kahall of Santa Sophia."

"Don't get fooled by the size of a Kahall. What goes on inside determines if a kahall is relevant or not."

I heard the anger in his voice after that comment. "I was not being critical of the kahall you grew up in."

"We will continue with the tour of the city in a few days," he replied and drove away from the kahall.

Chapter 10

"Noa Quadrant is the poorest quadrant in the city. The hovels you saw as we drove by are what people of this quadrant live in," Diakono Copperwith explained.

We had already driven by many of the small gray buildings that had to be the size of a single room. It was morning, and people were outside. They watched our car as we drove by and I remembered Diakono Copperwith telling me about the unbelievers that lived in this quadrant. I assumed that the festivals did not matter to these people at all.

I couldn't imagine a family living in such a place. The duplexes on the west side back home in Charlesville were at least twice the size of these hovels. Also, the duplexes were decorated and fixed up because those people cared about where they lived. The hovels were all the same color, drab and run-down.

"How can a family live in a place like that?" I asked.

"They are small. But Governor Henderson believed that every citizen of this city should have a home to live in, and he got approval from the Konseho of Kammbi to have these hovels built during his time in office."

"How long ago was that?"

Diakono Copperwith looked over at me. "Governor Henderson

was one of our most beloved governors. His term lasted eight years, beginning in the Year 181 A.O.A. Without him, the people of this quadrant would live on the streets."

"These hovels were built seventy years ago. Has the city ever tried to update them?"

We had driven through the entire quadrant in about fifteen minutes. It was mostly hovels and a couple of outdoor markets. I didn't see anyone out until we reached a large area that reminded me of Aliki Park except that it was mostly hills and thick grass, without many trees. Diakono Copperwith explained how Santa Sophia operated as we got out of car and began walking through the park. The Konseho of Kammbi appointed a governor every four years as well as a governing council. There were five members, one from each quadrant and the city operator. The Konseho of Kammbi formed this type of government after Oscar Ortega died and wanted to give the illusion that the people of the city could participate in how their government should operate.

However, the transition wasn't that easy. For many years, the power of the city had remained in the hands of the three families who helped build Santa Sophia after Oscar Ortega died—the Ortega, Carranza, and Merez families. Finally, the Konseho of Kammbi flexed its power and appointed Herman Henderson as governor, and that broke the control the three families had on the city.

"Governors after him made sure the basic upkeep of the hovels was maintained. Governor Henderson signed a law mandating it and that these residents don't pay for living expenses. The other governors after him have followed the law and done nothing else."

In the distance, a big, triangular-shaped item got my attention. There were people standing in front of it.

"That is called a shimmaro. The lights on the shimmaro start glowing today, and one light a day will burn out for the next thirty days until the Festival of Sinquinta, as a countdown in honor of Oscar Ortega's arrival here."

"I have never seen anything like that before," I said.

After walking for what seemed like several miles, the diakono and I gotten closer to the shimmaro. The lights were shaped into a triangle, and the shimmaro stood quite high from the ground. People were bowing in front of it, and I heard some singing as well.

"Not yet, Diondray," Diakono Copperwith said and gently pulled me away from where I was standing. "I will make sure that you get a chance to stand in front of the shimmaro."

We walked past the shimmaro, angling along its left side. However, I kept looking back to see how people dropped to their knees in front of it. The shimmaro seemed like it had a magnetic pull that drew them in. I felt that pull, and I wanted to go back and stare at it myself.

Diakono Copperwith led me quite a distance away from the shimmaro. I was starting to get tired from all this walking. I was out of shape. We stopped in a cluster of trees.

"Forgive me for making you walk so far. I wanted to get some distance from the shimmaro," Diakono Copperwith said as stood in front of me.

"Because?"

"The shimmaro is very important to us here in the city. However, it can be quite distracting."

I agreed with that comment. Distracting in a good way.

"I would like for you to read from one of your themilies here at the shimmaro."

"Why?" I replied. "My themilies are from my experiences back home in Charlesville."

"Oscar Ortega shared his knowledge with the Mayza tribe when he first arrived, and they accepted it. The people here will do the same with your themily."

It had been a while since I had read a themily. I did want to get in front of a crowd and read. I had never seriously thought I would do it here in Santa Sophia.

"I will."

The Diakono had a big smile across his face. "Be ready tomorrow. You will read after the first light is burnt out on the shimmaro."

* * *

I paced the area behind the shimmaro. It was twenty-nine days until the Festival of Sinquinta, and the first light on the shimmaro was going to burn out this evening. I had thought all day about what themily I was going to read to the people of this city. I had tried to write a new themily last night, and my mind raced for quite a while before I was able to come up with some words I thought would be suitable for these people to hear. I had finally decided I would read the new one today.

"Are you all right, Diondray?"

I looked over at Diakono Copperwith and saw his thin, reassuring smile. "I will be all right," I replied.

The diakono touched my shoulder when I paced in front of him. "You will do well."

I felt the heat from his long, thin hand, and I relaxed instantly. I stopped and faced him. At that moment, I had a quick thought about Trayvonne and realized that Diakono Copperwith had that same ability to reassure me just with his presence. "I will say a few words, and then my wife, Annalisa, will burn out the light. After she finishes, you will read your themily."

I nodded.

He shook his head in wonder. "I still can't believe that I will be alive when Oscar's prophecy will be fulfilled."

I followed him as we came in front of the shimmaro. I stood on his left side and looked at all the people who were right in front of us. They all had their heads bowed while being on their knees. Diakono Copperwith walked right up to them, and I knew he had complete control of the crowd.

"Raise your heads," he said, and the people followed his instruction. "We have begun the countdown until the Festival of Sinquinta and will tonight burn out the first light of the shimmaro. We know from the Book of Kammbi that these were the last days of Oscar Ortega's journey to these hills; in these days started the vision our Lord Kammbi had for this land. And every year since Oscar went to be with him, we have celebrated his trust in our Lord. Now, we have reached an opportunity we have never seen before. This year, the fulfillment of Kammbi's total vision will happen."

The people were transfixed, their eyes and faces rapt. "Annalisa, will you please burn out the first light?"

To my right, Annalisa walked toward her husband. She wore a long purple dress that flowed with the wind. Annalisa's hair flew up as she walked, and she had a motherly attractiveness that was appealing. I noticed a silver object in her right hand. I had no idea what it was.

Annalisa walked past Diakono Copperwith and went up to the shimmaro. She went to the bottom, right-hand corner and raised that silver object in front of the light. Seconds later, I heard a rush of wind coming from the object and It burnt out light instantly as the smoke rose into the air.

I turned to look back at the people. They all had their arms raised in the air. Then I heard a low, harmonious chant coming from them. It lasted only a few seconds as the people rose to their feet.

"We have a special event happening next," Diakono Copperwith said. "We will hear some words of wisdom from a person who has come from south of the Great Forest. While his words are not from the Book of Kammbi, Diondray Azur will share his wisdom with us and continue the tradition that Oscar Ortega started when he first arrived."

My hands shook as I stared down at the paper. I cleared my throat and began.

"Is a stranger always a stranger? Or can a stranger become a friend? Or do people here keep a stranger at arm's distance? Or do people here bring a stranger close enough to be embraced? Is love for a stranger the same as love for a friend or relative?"

Sweat dropped from my face to make several wet spots on my paper. I had never felt so nervous in reading a themily. I looked up and saw people with heads bowed and still on their knees. Were they accepting my words? Or were they being gracious to me because I was an outsider?

I was finished. I folded the paper and nodded at the diakono.

"Diondray has asked an important question. Is a stranger always a stranger? Well, I believe as a citizen of this city, we know how to welcome and make him a friend," Diakono Copperwith said as he stood next to me.

The people lifted their heads and rose to their feet. There were genuine smiles on their faces. My themily had been accepted.

Diakono Copperwith said a few closing words, and the people began leaving the area.

"Beautiful words, Diondray," Annalisa said. "I didn't believe the people would take your words. They were simple, direct and insightful. You could be the one to fulfill Oscar's Prophecy and I'm beginning to believe that all my years of reading the Book of Kammbi were not in vain."

Annalisa clasped my hands and bowed her head. I was speechless.

* * *

Four days passed after my visit to the shimmaro. I reread the Book of Kammbi, going over the part where Oscar first arrived in this area and shared the teachings of Kammbi with the Mayza tribe. The writer of Book 3 of the Baramesa didn't say how receptive the Mayza to those teachings. It seemed like they had already accepted them and in the next chapter started believing in Kammbi as their god.

I would have liked to know if they had really accepted Kammbi as their god so quickly. If so, what convinced them that Oscar's god could be their god as well? Had the people of this city accepted the words of my themily as easily as the Mayza tribe did for Oscar Ortega?

I started to close the book when Second Esperah Carranza entered the room. He was wearing a long black shirt with white trim on the collar and pants that were same color as the shirt. I had never seen him in an outfit like that before.

"Diakono Copperwith is in Santa Teresa with the morrim, and he wanted me to take you to the shimmaro," he said.

Santa Teresa was another city north of the Great Forest and southeast of Santa Sophia. I had read about it in Book 4 of the Baramesa. Oscar Ortega traveled there on his expedition and met the matriarch, Teresa, who was one of his first converts to believing in and following Kammbi.

"Does he leave Santa Sophia often?" I asked.

"He has recently. Diakono Copperwith is being prepared to become the next morrim of this kahall."

"He has not mentioned that at all."

"I can see that you are surprised by this news."

"I am."

"Before you came, Diondray, all the Second Esperahs met with the morrim. The morrim told us that he felt his time in the position was coming to an end, and he asked all of us which diakono we thought should be the next morrim. Eleven of the twelve second esperahs chose Diakono Copperwith."

"What about the one who didn't choose him?"

"That second esperah serves at another kahall."

I followed Second Esperah Carranza out of the room, wondering whether Diakono Copperwith really wanted to become the morrim of the kahall of Santa Sophia. What if he wanted to stay a diakono? Could he refuse becoming a morrim? Or had Kammbi chosen him? His words about "obedience" still rang in my ears.

We reached the parking lot, where a white bus was parked. The vehicle looked similar to the one I had ridden in when I left the airport after first arriving in Santa Sophia.

"It should take us about ten minutes to get to the shimmaro," Second Esperah Carranza said as we drove away.

I looked out the window, noticing the sun's descent. Night was quickly approaching. I wanted Second Esperah Carranza to continue with the conversation about Diakono Copperwith being prepared to become the morrim. But he remained quiet as we reached the marperia.

He parked on Oscar Ortega Boulevard and started to exit the bus. "I will return shortly."

I watched him walk toward the crowd in the marperia. I had no idea why he had stopped there or what he was doing. Moments later, Second Esperah Carranza had some of the crowd follow him to the bus.

"Please find a seat,' he said to the crowd behind him upon entering the autobus. "Diondray, I pick up people every evening during the last twenty days before the Festival of Sinquinta. Most of them come from the Enoshe and Noa Quadrants and have no other way to see the shimmaro. I make sure they get to see it every night until the festival."

The people were seated, and Second Esperah Carranza drove away from the marperia. I gained even more respect for him at that moment.

I glanced back at the people seated behind me on the bus. They were mostly families. I know Second Esperah Carranza had said they came from the Enoshe and Noa Quadrants and were poor, but I didn't get that kind of feeling from them. They were all dressed and groomed nicely. The children didn't have the look in their eyes of being less fortunate, like some I had seen in the west side back home. Maybe their version of poor was different from I what had seen.

We reached the shimmaro, and Second Esperah Carranza gathered the passengers off the bus. Some of them glanced at me as they exited. I noticed smiles on their faces in anticipation of seeing the shimmaro. I could tell how much seeing that huge light meant to them.

They followed behind him in a single line. I exited the bus and walked a little distance behind. Second Esperah Carranza led them through the crowd that was already standing at the shimmaro. I watched how those people moved out of the way for the autobus passengers. It was like they knew these people belonged in the very front of the shimmaro.

"Are you leaving?" I asked Second Esperah Carranza. He had almost walked by me.

"Yes, there are more people at the marperia," he replied over his shoulder.

I watched him walk away from the crowd back to the autobus. He reminded me of the CRG guards at that moment. They were devoted to their duty of protecting my family and the city. I had always admired their dedication to their job, and I was seeing that again in this man.

"Could you stand next to me?"

I turned around and saw a little boy with huge eyes that covered most of his face looking up at me. "Sure," I answered. "What's your name?"

"Antonio."

He stood and waited for me to stand next to him. Antonio's light brown skin and stringy dark brown hair were a striking contrast to my own features. But those eyes pulled me in, and I walked up a few steps to stand by him.

"I saw you on the autobus and believe that you are special," he told me very seriously.

Even though he was small, his tone was so serious it was almost intimidating. However, I didn't feel threatened by his demeanor.

"I know you are from south of the Great Forest," he continued. "I heard about you from Lady Patricia. She said you are the one to fulfill Oscar's prophecy. She is right."

"How do you know that?" I asked him.

"The Eternal Comforter told me."

"How did the Eternal Comforter tell you?"

Antonio pointed his left index finger at his heart. Then he moved that finger to the left side of his forehead. "The Eternal Comforter speaks to me in both places."

I looked at Antonio as he stared at the shimmaro. Even though four more lights were burnt out, signifying there were twenty-five days until the Festival of Sinquinta, I couldn't stop thinking about this child and his strong belief about who I was.

Chapter 11

It was eleven days until the Festival of Sinquinta. I had spent the last fourteen days going to the shimmaro with Second Esperah Carranza. I wanted to go to with him to see if I could talk to Antonio again. I accompanied him on his pickups at the marperia, hoping to see that child. I never saw him again. But his comments about the Eternal Comforter stayed with me. He spoke so earnestly about it. Did believing in Kammbi give children such conviction?

For the last four days, I had also reread Book 4 of the Baramesa. Book 4 records Teresa's account of Oscar Ortega's ministry when he arrived in the area now known as the city of Santa Teresa. Teresa was the matriarch of the tribe that ruled the area, and she wrote about Oscar's beliefs in the Eternal Comforter. He convinced her that the Eternal Comforter guided his every decision, and when she believed in Kammbi, Teresa would receive the gift of the Eternal Comforter into her own being as well.

Even though I had read Book 4 several times already and gotten the basic understanding that one received the Eternal Comforter as a gift for believing in and following Kammbi, I still didn't have a clear picture of when the gift of Eternal Comforter was supposed to come to you. I certainly didn't have him. Then again, I wasn't even sure I was a follower of Kammbi.

After breakfast, I walked over to Diakono Copperwith's office. He had returned from his teaching sessions with the morrim.

"How have the last few days with Second Esperah Carranza been?" he asked as I sat down in front of his desk.

"I've learned a lot about him in the past few days."

"That he drives a bus." Diakono Copperwith gave a smile after that comment.

"I will admit that surprised me," I replied. "Also, that he picks up people from the marperia each day until the Festival of Sinquinta."

"He has been doing that a long time. It has truly been a benefit to the kahall."

"I would agree with that assessment. After one of those pickups, I had a little boy named Antonio stand next to me at the shimmaro. He knew I was from south of the Great Forest and said I was a special person."

Diakono Copperwith raised his eyebrows in anticipation of what I was going to say next.

"I asked Antonio how he knew. He said the Eternal Comforter told him."

Diakono Copperwith gave a bigger smile and nodded.

"How did he receive the Eternal Comforter? He's only a child."

"He believes and follows Kammbi."

"So did he receive it as soon as he confessed his belief in Kammbi? Or did his parents do that for him?"

"You should have read that every believer and follower receives the gift of the Eternal Comforter once they truly believe and follow him."

"How would a child know to believe in a god so easily on his own?"

"Children can believe in Kammbi much easier than adults. They have not been tainted by the harsh realities of adult life. Kammbi himself speaks about this in the Book 2 of the Ryianza: 'Every tongue will speak for him or herself. They will believe and follow me with their own heart and mind.'"

"Kammbi was talking about the Eternal Comforter in that chapter?"

"Yes."

"That doesn't answer how a child like that would *know* with such belief. His parents are believers and followers of Kammbi. I assume he has no other choice but to believe in and follow Kammbi."

Diakono Copperwith stood up from his desk and looked at me with his reassuring smile. "Come," he said.

* * *

We left Diakono Copperwith's office and walked over to the main sanctuary of the kahall. I had not spent any time in the sanctuary since being in Santa Sophia. I knew the morrim taught the congregation there every seventh day. But neither the diakono nor Second Esperah Carranza had brought me to those teachings. I guessed Diakono Copperwith thought the time was right for me to go there today.

I followed him through the main entrance, and instead of turning right to go to my room, I stayed left and entered the main sanctuary.

It was enormous. The main sanctuary alone seemed bigger than all of Kahall Thirty-Seven, where I'd stopped with Diakono Copperwith. I scanned the entire room and noticed the red and green pillars coming down from the ceiling. The glass on each side of the sanctuary had images imprinted on it. At the front of the sanctuary was a podium that stood in the center of a stage.

Diakono Copperwith led me to a front-row seat on the left side of the sanctuary. I felt the eyes of the congregation on me as I walked by. It was not a large congregation, and only half the rows were filled. I wondered if this was a special kind of teaching session. From my room's window, I could see the crowd for the morrim's teachings every seventh day. It was always bigger than this.

Moments later, I saw a small man wearing a white shawl with red trim walking to the podium. He seemed frail and gaunt. But his piercing stare at Diakono Copperwith and myself when he reached the podium held my attention. I knew this was the morrim.

I looked at Diakono Copperwith, who sat to my right, and observed a distant look on his face.

"I want to thank you all for coming," the morrim said. "As you know, we are heading toward the Festival of Sinquinta in celebration of Oscar Ortega's obedience to our Lord.

"However, I didn't come to teach this morning. I have a special announcement. They say that change can come in an instant. I must admit I have never liked that saying, because when you are believer and follower of Kammbi, you should never have to worry about change. Kammbi is constant. Well, I have learned even at this advanced stage of my life that change *can* come suddenly, and we must be able to react appropriately."

The morrim's full head of cloud-white hair and the wrinkled skin on his face made me think of Trayvonne's grandfather, Scarro. I didn't know exactly why. I thought the morrim had the same kind of presence and command of the room that Scarro did, even though they were both elderly.

Diakono Copperwith moved in his seat. Was something wrong?

"Today, I have to announce that my message at the Festival of Sinquinta will be my last as the morrim of the kahall of Santa Sophia. I have heard the Eternal Comforter speak to me, and my thirty-two years of being the morrim has come to an end.

"It is time for a new morrim. The diakonos and I have selected Diakono Malcolm Copperwith to become the new morrim of the kahall of Santa Sophia."

Diakono Copperwith looked like he had just lost a relative. The color in his face was gone, and I could sense that he was not happy about the announcement.

The morrim left the podium, and the congregation clapped for several minutes after he exited. Why was Diakono Copperwith not happy?

* * *

I didn't see Diakono Copperwith for the next three days. After the Morrim's announcement, Second Esperah Carranza told me that he was with the morrim and the other diakonos for prayer sessions.

I tried to find out from Second Esperah Carranza if there was something wrong. I knew the diakono was not happy about the announcement.

Second Esperah Carranza explained how becoming the morrim had been Diakono Copperwith's main goal since he arrived at the kahall. While he never campaigned to become the morrim, everyone knew he was next in line for it. So the announcement was no thrill to him; it was expected. Besides, there was no reason for a celebration because of the announcement: being morrim of the largest and most prominent kahall in the city carried a huge responsibility. That required someone with the proper personality and temperament for being a morrim. So Diakono Copperwith wasn't unhappy, he explained; he was just appropriately serious.

I appreciated Second Esperah Carranza's explanation, but I didn't buy it. I knew something was wrong with Diakono Copperwith, and I had to find out what.

Diakono Copperwith came to my room later that evening. I'd just had dinner, and I was going to start writing a new themily when he arrived. He still had the same distant look on his face I'd seen after the morrim's announcement.

"Diondray, I have seen in the short time we have gotten to know each other that you have a gift of perception. So I decided to come talk to you about what has happened."

He was wearing a white shawl with red trim just like the morrim had worn at the announcement. Because of his height, it seemed that the diakono looked down at me like a father would his son.

"After the Festival of Sinquinta, I will be leaving Santa Sophia with you as you begin your own expedition. If you are the one to fulfill Oscar's prophecy, then you must travel throughout the entire land just like Oscar did."

"What?"

"The thing I have wanted all my life has come. But Kammbi had other plans for me."

Diakono Copperwith raised his shoulders and corrected his posture. He was trying to make peace with this decision.

I was trying to understand what he was saying. "You cannot be morrim."

"Correct."

"How do you know?"

"The Eternal Comforter has said so."

"How can a spirit tell you to turn away from the one thing you have wanted all your life? That doesn't make sense to me."

He almost smiled. "Your comment has validated what the Eternal Comforter has told me."

"My comment?"

"Your lack of understanding of what the Eternal Comforter is has a bearing on this decision. If you are to become the one who fulfills Oscar's prophecy, then you must understand how important the Eternal Comforter will be in your life from this day forward."

I paced the room while Diakono Copperwith stood near the door.

"Let's go to the shimmaro. I have someone else for you to meet."

I stopped pacing and looked at him. "Someone else."

"Diondray, I'm not the only one going with you. There is another person who will join us."

I followed him out of the room and began wondering who this other person could be.

* * *

Only eight lights still burned on the shimmaro. It seemed like time had gotten faster as we came closer to the Festival of Sinquinta. However, my thoughts were not on those lights. Diakono Copperwith remained silent during the entire drive to the shimmaro. He was trying to come to grips with not being able to do the one thing he had wanted to do all of his life.

Also, I was going to meet another person who would join us when we left Santa Sophia. If I was going to follow in Oscar's footsteps, why would the diakono and this mystery person need to go with me? Oscar traveled only with Reuel the leopard during his expedition. Was this another suggestion from the Eternal Comforter?

Diakono Copperwith left me standing near the shimmaro for a good bit of time. I felt the chill of the night go through my clothes, and I realized I would probably never get used to the weather in Santa Sophia.

I was watching the people bow in front of the shimmaro when Diakono Copperwith returned with a female companion. She had long, dark-brown hair, fair skin, and a sharp chin. The woman was striking.

"I'm Maisa Merez," she said and extended her hand to me.

I reached for her hand and shook it. It was smooth and feminine.

"I have heard quite a bit about you, Diondray Azur," she continued. "I'm joining you on your expedition."

Maisa's smile that drew me into her gaze. I felt nervous all of sudden and turned away to look at Diakono Copperwith so my mind would have to focus on something else.

"She will be spending the remaining days up to the Festival of Sinquinta at the kahall. There is a lot of preparation to do for this expedition, and Maisa's experience in traveling both north and south of the Great Forest will be greatly appreciated," Diakono Copperwith said.

"You have traveled south of the Great Forest?" I asked.

Maisa laughed softly. "Yes, I've been to Adrian and Walter's Grove. Not your hometown of Charlesville."

"I would never have thought anyone from north of the Great Forest would have traveled to the other side. I'm really impressed."

"Well, my great-uncle did it first in our family. I want to continue that tradition."

"Who was your great uncle?"

"Marco Philip Merez. Patriarch of the Merez family."

"Marco Phillip Merez?" The name sounded vaguely familiar, but why?

"The Merez family has always been the overlooked family in the city's history. Pedro married Niomi Ortega, and our families have been linked ever since. However, the Ortega family has been more much visible and prominent than my family," she replied and smiled at me again.

Diakono Copperwith cleared his throat. "Well, Diondray, I wanted you to meet Maisa. You will be seeing a lot of her over the next few days. You two have a lot in common and many stories to share."

"Nice to meet you, Diondray," she said and shook my hand again.

"Likewise," I replied.

Diakono Copperwith and Maisa began to walk away, and I noticed she was wearing a sun-yellow dress that flattered her figure. I thought of Travyone and knew he would have said something about her ample backside. I chuckled at that thought and realized how much I missed him.

Chapter 12

I got Second Esperah Carranza to drop me off at the marperia this morning. We were seven days away from the Festival of Sinquinta. And I had more questions about fulfilling Oscar's prophecy than answers. That Diakono Copperwith and Maisa were leaving their city like I had done with mine confused me.

I had my paper and pencil with me as I sat on a bench across from Kammbi's statue. I was finishing a new themily, and I kept staring at the statue. Kammbi's arms were extended wide, inviting all to come to him. At what price? Taking a man from his city in order to follow a set of beliefs he didn't fully grasp? Forcing another man to give up one thing he wanted to do in order to help a stranger fulfill a prophecy he didn't fully embrace? And bringing an attractive woman along as well—pulling her out of her world and her family for what?

I could not write anything. It seemed that Kammbi put those who believed and followed him through a lot. And yet, somehow I had become committed. I admitted to myself that I did not want to return to Charlesville. I felt I had to see this journey through.

* * *

For the next two days, I looked for Maisa at the kahall. Every time I left my room to go to the shimmaro with Second Esperah Carranza,

I hoped I would see her. I didn't. I was disappointed.

Second Esperah Carranza told me she was helping Diakono Copperwith with the transition of leaving the kahall. Diakono Copperwith had said she would be quite busy right up to the Festival of Sinquinta. Since we were five days away, I had to accept that I might not see her until then.

I searched through the book again to see if the writers mentioned the Merez family. I only remembered reading about the Ortega and Carranza families in the Book of Kammbi. I wondered why the Merez family was not mentioned at all.

Second Esperah Carranza explained to me after breakfast that since Marco Phillip Merez had married Niomi Ortega after Oscar died, the Merez family could not be added into the Book of Kammbi. The morrim of the kahall of Santa Sophia at the time of Oscar's death proclaimed the Book of Kammbi could not be changed until the fulfillment of Oscar's prophecy. Because of that proclamation, the Merez family had always been the invisible family in the city's history, overlooked for their contribution to Santa Sophia.

It didn't seemed right that one of the three prominent families in Santa Sophia would not be added to the Book of Kammbi. Had Marco Phillip Merez traveled south of Great Forest after Oscar Ortega in order to get his family name recognized? Could it be that Maisa was doing the same thing with Diakono Copperwith and myself?

Whatever her reasons were for traveling with us, I hoped I would get to know her. I hadn't felt this way since Mara. Trayvonne had tried to get me to pursue women with him after our relationship had ended, but I was not ready for another woman at that time.

But I don't know how Maisa felt about me. And it could all be wishful thinking on my part. Women were mysterious, as Trayvonne would tell me. I might think she was interested in me but quickly find out that wasn't true. And was I really ready for another relationship myself?

Well, I wanted to see her at the shimmaro tonight. I wanted to get to know more about her and learn why she had really decided to leave Santa Sophia with us.

* * *

I didn't see Maisa at the shimmaro. However, I got invited to the morrim's feast the following day by Diakono Copperwith, who told me she would be there. The diakono said the morrim wanted me at the feast, and my presence at the dinner would be an historic event: I would be the first person from south of the Great Forest to be a guest at the morrim's feast. I would never have thought anything I did would be historical.

As Second Esperah Carranza explained to me, the kahall was putting on a huge feast that would be attended by the morrim, diakonos, and other invited guests. The morrim wanted to have a meal where he could express his gratitude to the others and allow the diakonos to express their gratefulness as well. Also, the morrim wanted the feast to be a time where everyone was relaxed and could enjoy each other without the protocol of the kahall. The morrim and other diakonos wanted to express their gratitude for Diakono Copperwith's service and wish him well.

I was in Diakono Copperwith's office when he told me about the feast, and I sensed he had come to grips with the fact he was leaving. His confident, reassuring voice from when I first met him had returned. I guessed having a strong belief in the Eternal Comforter could make you accept a decision that you truly didn't want.

I got dressed after returning from the diakono's office. I was started to wonder if maybe the Eternal Comforter had been guiding me all along. I knew I wasn't a believer in Kammbi. But I'd had no idea I would be coming to this city. I'd had no idea that I had a family member who believed in Kammbi and secretly came here to set up my arrival. It seemed that everything in these past months had been put together beyond my control, all in order for Oscar's prophecy to be fulfilled. I had thought I was in such control of my life when I moved out of my family's home. I had declared my independence. Or was it my declared independence that had led me here and on my way to another life I never knew existed?

* * *

Dusk had arrived when I entered the main sanctuary for the morrim's feast. I could see the coming of the night through one of the windows on the right side of the sanctuary. The morrim and diakonos were sitting at a long table covered by a red cloth. I was looking for Maisa. She had not arrived yet. I hoped she had not been asked to do something else.

Second Esperah Frances Oliva led me to my seat. She looked like a little girl to me instead of a second esperah. Her perfectly round face and cream-colored skin projected an innocence I easily detected. I knew that Second Esperah Carranza was doing his duties by picking up people at the marperia in order to take them to the shimmaro. His presence at the morrim's feast would have been welcomed.

I sat on the left side of the table, one seat away from the end. Diakono Copperwith was seated next to me on my right, and there were three other Diakonos and the morrim seated across from us. They all gave me a polite, quick smile and then faced the other end of the table.

Second Esperah Oliva was joined by two more second esperahs as they put plates in front of each person at the table. They began serving sliced bread and pouring juice into each glass. They seemed to have a peace about them and were totally focused on doing what they were supposed to do for the feast.

"Thank you all for coming," the morrim said. "We only have four days left before the Festival of Sinquinta, and I wanted this feast to happen today instead of the day before the festival."

I scanned the table and saw the diakonos nod at the morrim's comment. I noticed they all had the same cream-colored skin and realized how my dark-brown skin stood out amongst them.

"As you know, I had selected Diakono Malcolm Copperwith to replace me as morrim of this kahall," the morrim continued. "But as soon as I made that decision, I heard from the Eternal Comforter that there was a different path for Diakono Copperwith."

"How do you know that?" I blurted out.

The morrim stared at me momentarily. "When you trust in Kammbi, you will receive the gift of the Eternal Comforter. I understand you have read the Book of Kammbi, Diondray Azur."

I felt all the eyes of the table on me. "With all due respect, I have read the Book of Kammbi—several times, in fact. But this Eternal Comforter concept is still giving me trouble. How do you know that a voice inside of you can tell Diakono Copperwith that he can't be morrim of the kahall? How could it keep him from the thing he most desired?"

"I can tell you haven't read the Ryianza," one of the diakonos seated across from me replied, looking down his long nose. "Kammbi said in Book 7 that he would always be with his people, even after he sacrificed himself for all of us. The Eternal Comforter is the gift he left us so that we could always remain connected with him."

"Before we get too deep in conversation, let's eat," the morrim said. "Diondray, your question is why Diakono Copperwith is going with you."

The second esperahs brought the rest of the food and served us. I was thinking about the Diakono's comment when I looked up from my plate and saw Maisa coming to the table. She was wearing a simple white dress with pink trim. Her hair fell just above the shoulders, and she had a presence that got everyone's attention.

"Better late than never," the diakono with the sharp nose commented.

The morrim gave that diakono with a sharp look. The diakono dropped his head and returned to eating.

"Thanks for the compliment, Diakono Alvarez," Maisa replied and sat to my left, at the end of the table.

"Maisa, thank you for coming," the morrim said. "And all your help in these past few days has been appreciated by all of us."

She smiled at the morrim after his comment. I could feel my legs shaking under the table. I wanted to get up and pace around the table. But I couldn't.

"Diondray asked a question. Why would the Eternal Comforter keep Diakono Copperwith from becoming the next morrim of this kahall? Also, hasn't the Eternal Comforter kept you from something as well, Maisa?" the morrim said.

"It is not what we want, but what Kammbi wants for us," Maisa replied and looked at me.

"That sounds like protocol. Of course we want to do what Kammbi wants. Does that convince our visitor?" Diakono Alvarez replied.

I liked Diakono Alvarez after that comment. He had an independent streak in him. I wondered what got him to become a diakono.

"Why don't you tell us?" another diakono with a deep voice asked.

Diakono Alvarez was quick to answer. "Do you know how many believers and followers of Kammbi tell me they want to do what he wants? After every service, I get prayer requests from our congregation saying they want me to pray for them about doing what Kammbi wants. Then a hard choice comes to them from the Eternal Comforter, and they want another prayer session from me on what to do. Didn't you just pray about doing what Kammbi wants? He just gave it to you, and now you want me to pray for you so you won't have to do it."

I watched all the diakonos and the morrim nod in agreement. Their nodding told me they'd all had the same experience with the congregation.

"Obedience is the hardest thing to do, even when you want to," Maisa said.

The morrim smiled at her comment and replied, "That's why we celebrate the Festival of Sinquinta every year. Oscar Ortega obeyed immediately and without question. And that's why Diakono Copperwith and Maisa must do what the Eternal Comforter wants. Obedience brings the reward."

After the morrim's comment, I realized what my issue has been all of these years.

Chapter 13

The day had arrived. The Festival of Sinquinta would begin in a few short hours. I had spent the last three days after the morrim's feast in my room rereading the Book of Kammbi and finishing a new themily.

Now I had to pack up my stuff, and it hit me that when I left this room, I would never come back to it. I had gotten used to the big window, the comfortable bed, and the three meals served to me by Second Esperah Carranza. It would all be missed.

I heard a knock at my door before I could continue to reminisce about my time here at the kahall.

"Ready to go," Maisa said as I opened the door.

She was wearing an orange blouse with dark blue pants. Her hair was placed in a ponytail and accentuated the roundness of her face. She was striking.

"Ready."

"From this point, Diondray, we will spend a lot time together." She smiled as I gathered my suitcase.

I followed her out of the room and stepped forward into the next phase of my life.

We arrived at the Ortega Hills about fifteen minutes later. Maisa and I chatted quite a bit on the drive, and we learned a little bit more about each other's families. She still had this mysterious presence. But I was starting to get comfortable being around her.

The Ortega Hills were magnificent. I thought back to when I had first seen them with Diakono Copperwith. They gave off a peaceful vibe that made Maisa and I stop talking as we got closer. It seemed like those hills were endless, cutting deep into the horizon.

"We have a spot all ready for us," Maisa said after we got out of the automobile. "The morrim made sure we have one of the best spots to see the entire festival."

"That was kind of him."

"He didn't do it to be kind."

"What?"

"You are going to be a part of the Festival of Sinquinta."

Maisa looked over at me after that comment. If she wanted to see surprise on my face, she got it. Who had decided I was going to be a part of the festival?

"If you are going to fulfill Oscar's prophecy, then you have to be a part of the festival. Remember from your reading of the Book of Kammbi, Oscar was a stranger when he first arrived amongst the Mayza tribe. He attended the tribe's celebrations and spoke to them in that arena. Since you are Oscar's second coming, in a sense, you must follow the same path."

We reached an area where a hill was divided into two sections. Both sides of the hill were decorated in red and green paper that went to the top.

I followed Maisa on a walkway that was created by a division of the hill. What would I be doing in this festival?

Maisa led me to the end of the walkway. We walked up the side of the hill for a short ways. There was a cave created in that part of hill. Maisa and I sat at the cave's entrance. I looked out and saw the people coming onto the walkway.

"Most of our city will be here shortly," Maisa said.

"What will I be doing?"

She gave a wan smile. "You should know. You have read Baramesa Book 1, when Oscar Ortega arrived in this area."

"I'm going to eat amongst the Mayza tribe?"

She nodded and said, "Let's look at the people of this city, one last time."

Maisa turned away from me to watch the people coming into the area. I didn't know what I was going to do, and I got up to pace.

"Please sit down!" Maisa said.

I didn't want to, but I didn't have much room to pace. The area inside the cave was tight.

"Please sit down. The Festival of Sinquinta will be starting soon."

I returned to my seat and didn't look at Maisa. I gazed out at the people coming onto the walkway and trying to get seated on each side of the hill. She was not kidding about the entire city coming to the festival.

"Are you okay?" she asked and touched my left shoulder.

"Yes," I replied. But I did not look at her.

"I didn't mean to scare you. I just thought since you had been here for some time that you had adjusted to our city."

"I didn't know I was going to participate today."

"Please look at me," she replied. "I was told you had read the Book of Kammbi. At least the seven books of the Baramesa, and you knew Oscar Ortega's entire story. So I thought you would know that you were going to be a part of the Festival of Sinquinta."

"How would I know that?" I asked and turned to face her.

She lowered her eyes with a remorseful look on her face. "You are right. You are a stranger. I should have not expected you to know our ways, even if you have read our book. I'm always going forward without thinking things through."

Before I could respond to her comment, I heard a loud sound in the distance. I looked out at the people who were still coming into the hill. But I could not tell where that sound came from.

"The horn will play for a while until the morrim of the kahall of Santa Sophia arrives," Maisa remarked.

I heard the sound again. This time it was louder. The horn had a low pitch and was deep. I thought I felt the cave shake after it played.

The horn got louder as I saw five men coming onto the walkway. The men were dressed in red and green. Their shirts and pants were blood red with green stripes on the sleeves, wrists, and pant legs. They were all about the same height and size. I could only tell the difference between the men because the first one of their group had cloud-white hair like the morrim, while the other men all had a distinct feature of their own.

"Diondray, those men represent the elders of the Mayza tribe that Oscar Ortega met when he first arrived," Maisa said. She had leaned over and said it in my ear because the horn had drowned out all the noise.

"Am I going to join them?"

"Yes."

I watched the men reach the end of the walkway. They were just below us, and I had no idea what I was going to do with them.

* * *

The morrim and the diakonos arrived on the walkway. Diakono Copperwith was the tallest of the diakonos and stood right behind the morrim.

They were all dressed in their white shawls with red trim, and all the people focused their attention on them as they walked toward the men who represented the elders of the Mayza tribe.

Maisa touched my shoulder and pointed to an area at the end of the walkway behind the elders.

I looked and saw a small table with a pitcher and a plate of cherries. The morrim reached the table and stood on the right side of it. The diakonos stood behind the elders, who were sitting on the ground.

"Welcome to the Festival of Sinquinta," the morrim announced. His voice carried throughout the area. I didn't know if he was wearing a microphone or not. "We are here for another year to celebrate Oscar Ortega's journey from Guadharra to these hills that bear his surname."

I cut my eyes to look at the people. Everybody seemed intently focused on the morrim's words.

"His journey took place two hundred and fifty years ago. It is still relevant today. And I would add now more than ever. Because Oscar trusted Kammbi when he told him to leave his homeland, we have received the reward of Oscar's obedience."

Maisa finally moved her hand off my shoulder. I shot a look at her, and she gave me a reassuring smile.

"Diakono Alvarez, please read from our beloved book," the morrim continued.

Diakono Alvarez stood on the left side from the morrim, behind the Mayza tribe member furthest away from Maisa and myself. I recognized that sharp nose from the morrim's feast. He had the Book of Kammbi in his right hand.

Diakono Alvarez opened the book and said, "Oscar arrived on the twenty-first day in the month of Aym. He came to an area of the hills where an opening was created and met the elders of the Mayza tribe for the first time."

The elders rose and walked to the table where the Morrim gave them a stalk of cherries and a glass of cherry juice.

"Oscar and his companion, Reuel, stood in front of the elders and told them about Kammbi. He spoke about Kammbi's sacrifice for all of humanity in order that all people could have a relationship with Abbahim," Diakono Alvarez continued.

I heard a loud growl, and that turned my focus away from the diakonos and the elders. The people began to murmur as a leopard arrived on the walkway.

"Here comes Reuel, Oscar's faithful companion," Diakono Alvarez said.

But the leopard ran past the Diakonos and the elders. It came up the hill toward Maisa and I in the ridge.

"Reuel, stop!" Maisa yelled.

The leopard ignored her plea and came straight toward me. I wanted to move, but my body was frozen. I could only stare at the menacing look of the leopard when it leapt toward me.

I felt the cat's leathery skin against my face and upper body. Reuel knocked me over . . . gently. I shivered all over, but I embraced the leopard.

"That is why today's Festival of Sinquinta is different than all the other ones before it," the morrim said.

Reuel got up off of me, and I stood while everyone was looking at us. Their faces were bewildered, and it seemed to dawn on them all at the same time that I was the one to fulfill Oscar's prophecy.

* * *

"Come, Diondray Azur," the morrim said.

I walked down from the cave, and Reuel joined me. I looked down at the leopard. It seemed to have a smile on its face. I would usually have been frightened of such an animal. But I'd lost any fear I had of this big cat after it jumped on me.

"Please sit in front of these men," the morrim continued.

I obeyed his instructions, and Reuel sat next to me. The elders stared at me while holding the glass of juice and cherries. I wanted to look away, but I felt an energy that made me look at them.

I received a glass of juice and a stalk of cherries from the morrim. I held up the glass and looked at the redness of the juice. I had to focus my attention on something besides everyone staring at me.

"Diondray and the elders, please hold up your glasses."

We did.

"Now take a bite of the cherries."

The cherries were sweet and delicious. I swallowed them rather quickly and wanted some more.

"Now take a sip of the juice."

The cherry juice was bitter, and I wanted to spit it out of my mouth. Quite a difference from the cherries I had just eaten.

"Pour the rest of the juice on the ground."

I poured out the juice and heard the splash of it hitting the ground.

"We have celebrated Kammbi's sacrifice for all of us. The juice poured on the ground represents the blood he shed for our acts of passha. We can never repay him for his sacrifice. But we can always recognize and honor what our Lord did for humanity."

I rubbed my tongue across my teeth in order to get the bitter taste of cherry juice out of my mouth. I wondered if that juice was bitter because of Kammbi's sacrifice.

"This Festival of Sinquinta is different from all of the others. For the first time, we have someone from south of the Great Forest here with us. And you all saw how Reuel, a seventh generation descendant of Oscar's companion, approached him. No leopard has ever done that in all the years I have led this festival."

The diakonos left their position behind the elders and came up to Reuel and me.

"I must say on this day that our Lord has honored his word," the morrim said. "We have the person who will fulfill Oscar's prophecy here with us."

The diakonos placed their hands on my shoulders.

"I have believed in and followed our Lord a long time," the morrim said. "I must admit even I had my doubts about this prophecy written in the Book of Kammbi. However, with the events that have happened since Diondray Azur's arrival into our city, my belief in him has been strengthened more than ever. I will finally live in a world where everybody will believe and follow in Kammbi."

I heard the people clapping. I couldn't see them because the diakonos surrounded me.

"The diakonos will bless Diondray Azur as he begins his journey in the fulfillment of Oscar's prophecy."

A deep, resonant voice read out words I almost knew by heart. "Because of your obedience in leaving your homeland to come to a new land, I will continue to make your name great. Even though you have lost a child due to your act of passha, you will have a descendant who will unite the entire land. And the people will believe that Kammbi is the Lord of all. Those who have always believed in me and those who didn't believe in me will create a new people, establishing peace and sanctification throughout this land."

I bowed my head as Diakono Copperwith read the words.

"Now with the blessing received, we will end this ceremony with the elders and their music," the morrim said.

The diakonos moved their hands away from my shoulders and returned to their positions. I looked up and saw the elders rise from their seats. They turned away from me as the horn played again. Reuel snuggled next to my thigh, and I knew what my destiny had become.

Thanks for reading Diondray's Discovery, the first book of The Diondray Chronicles and joining him on his adventure in Kammbia. If you enjoyed it? Diondray's adventures continue in:

Diondray's Journey, Book 2 of The Diondray Chronicles
Diondray's Roundabout, Book 3 and the final book of The Diondray Chronicles

Ciscoe's Dance is a new novel set in Kammbia that takes place after the events of The Diondray Chronicles. Coming in the Fall of 2020.

Also, I have released Marion's 25, the first non-fiction title of my favorite 25 books. Avid readers should be able to find some new book recommendations to add to your ever-growing TBR List!

If you want to keep up with all things Kammbia, then go to Marion's webpage: https://marion-hill.com/entry-into-kammbia/

Or you can connect with Marion here:

Blog: https://marion-hill.com/

Email: marion@marion-hill.com

Instagram: https://www.instagram.com/?hl=en

Goodreads:
https://www.goodreads.com/author/show/8202665.Marion_Hill

Bookbub: https://www.bookbub.com/profile/marion-hill-e4d3343b-634b-45e9-bcdf-294c03430436

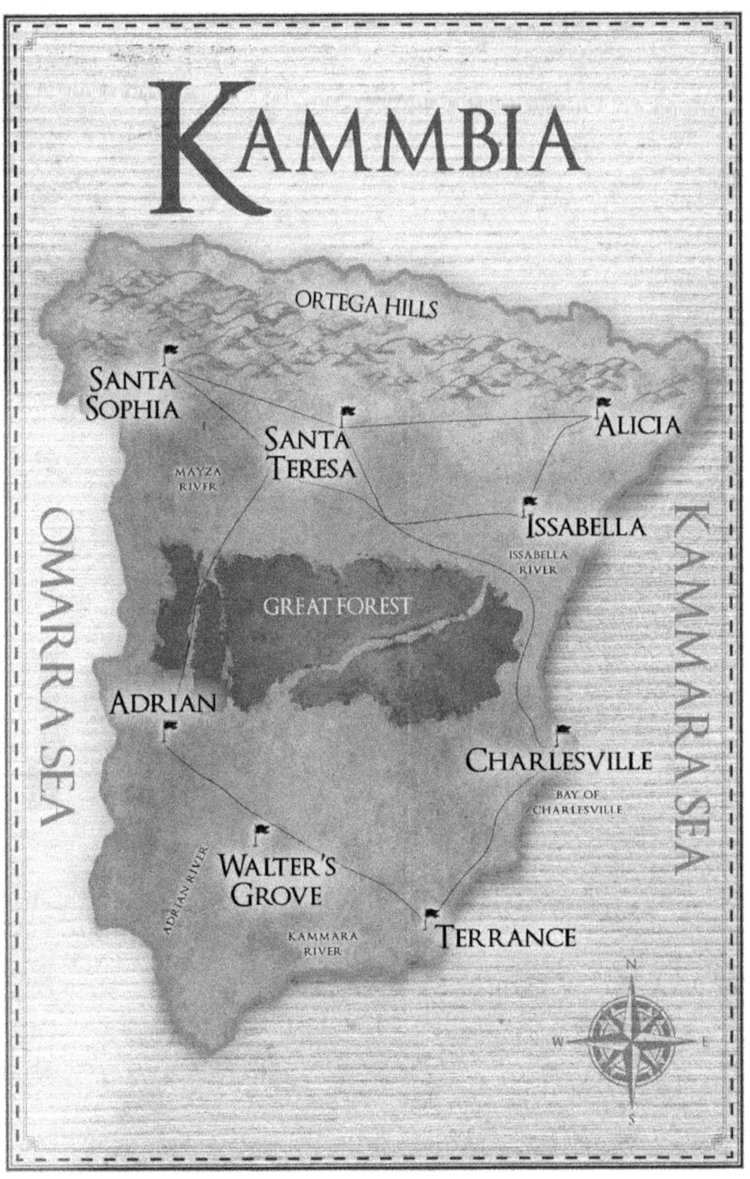
KAMMBIA
ORTEGA HILLS
SANTA SOPHIA
SANTA TERESA
ALICIA
MAYZA RIVER
ISSABELLA
ISSABELLA RIVER
GREAT FOREST
OMARRA SEA
KAMMARA SEA
ADRIAN
CHARLESVILLE
BAY OF CHARLESVILLE
ADRIAN RIVER
WALTER'S GROVE
KAMMARA RIVER
TERRANCE
N
W
E
S